Friends Needed

WHILE SHE WAITED for the laptop to power up, Morgan (Mo) started thinking about the fight with Jenna and Stacia again. She felt a dry lump form in the back of her throat. *How could they have turned out to be so horrible?* she wondered. Mo had been trying to put Jenna's comment about being "a project" out of her mind, but it was impossible not to think about it. Had Jenna and Stacia ever been real friends to Mo or had they always thought of her as some sort of challenge, like a makeover show or something? Mo swallowed hard, but the lump wouldn't go away. She opened a Web page and typed in the address of Wallace Emerson Middle School. Not sure what else to do, Mo decided to look around on the school Web site and see if she could come up with some sort of friend-meeting plan.

The Friendship Experiment

The Friendship Experiment

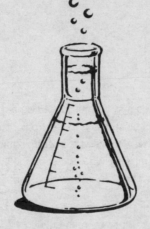

by Brandi Dougherty

Scholastic Inc.

New York Toronto London Auckland Sydney
Mexico City New Delhi Hong Kong Buenos Aires

ISBN-13: 978-0-545-07929-7
ISBN-10: 0-545-07929-2

12 11 10 9 8 7 6 5 4 3 2 1   9 10 11 12 13 14/0

Printed in the U.S.A.

First printing, February 2009

For Monica

—B. D.

The Friendship Experiment

CHAPTER 1
The Haircut

MORGAN RANG JENNA HALSTROM'S doorbell and instantly regretted it. She even turned around to face the street, like she was looking for an escape route.

"Hey, Mo." Jenna's twin brother Joey's blond head peeked out the front door. Mo's stomach dropped into her shoes. She was so nervous about seeing Jenna and her other BFF, Stacia Rogers, she had completely forgotten about Joey. He was so cute and always really nice.

"Hi, Joey, how's your summer been?" Mo managed to ask.

"Pretty sweet. I just can't believe it's already over," he answered, stepping aside to let Mo in.

"I know. It's crazy," Mo replied as she brushed by him, feeling her stomach jump up to her head this time.

"Oh, my goodness, Morgan Solas!" Jenna's mom's shrill voice exploded from the kitchen doorway. "Look at your hair! I thought you were growing your hair out this year, too?" She looked confused.

"I think it looks good," Joey mumbled as he ducked past Jenna's mom and into the kitchen. "See you later!" he called backward.

"Hi, Mrs. Halstrom," Mo whispered. "Yeah, well, I . . ." She nervously touched the edge of her freshly cut dark brown bob.

Jenna's mom wiped her hands on the dish towel she was carrying and turned Mo in a circle to look at her hair. *It's short all the way around,* Mo almost said, but thought better of it.

Jenna's mom let out a soft sigh. "Well, go on up — the girls are expecting you."

Mo had cut her hair while in her old hometown of

Maplewood with her old BFF, Libby (not "old" as in former or one-time BFF, more like all-time or longest-running BFF). Libby's aunt Sara was studying to be a hairstylist and had needed to practice her short bob, so Libby and Mo had volunteered to be hair models. It had been so much fun — the anticipation of a new look and letting Sara style it a million ways. They had even spent the afternoon dressing up in different outfits and taking pictures. But now that Jenna's mom had responded the way she did, Mo knew she was in trouble.

At the beginning of the summer, Jenna and Stacia had decided that they should all grow their hair out over the summer and start seventh grade with it exactly two inches below their shoulders. The problem was that Jenna and Stacia looked like they could be twins. They were the same average height (not too short and not too tall) and size (not too big and not too small), both had the same long, shiny, medium-blond hair with lighter blond highlights and bright blue eyes. Mo was definitely the odd girl out in the group. She had dark brown hair and hazel eyes and was at least six inches taller than Jenna and Stacia, though sometimes she felt six *feet* taller. Jenna and Stacia always looked totally put together, but Mo had big feet and skinny legs and was constantly tripping or spilling something on herself.

"You're just going through an awkward phase, honey," Mo's mother would say. "You'll grow into yourself, you'll see." But Mo felt like she was getting more awkward as time went on.

Mo's hair had been a little shorter (and frizzier for that matter) than Jenna and Stacia's at the time of the decision, but Jenna had said, "Don't worry, Mo. If you eat lots of protein over the summer and use that shampoo I gave you, you might only be, like, a quarter of an inch off from us. We can't do much about the color, unless your mom will let you dye it, but at least the length will be right."

So, Mo climbed the stairs to Jenna's bedroom like she was climbing to her doom. Spending time with Libby in Maplewood, doing all the things they loved to do — horseback riding, apple picking, swimming in the pond, and feeding the cows on Libby's farm — had made Mo realize that she wasn't totally herself with Jenna and Stacia. In fact, when Libby had talked about coming to Kirkland for a visit later in the fall, Mo had been embarrassed to think of Libby meeting her friends. She couldn't exactly figure out why, but something about them and the way Mo felt when she was with them just didn't feel right.

Mo's clammy hand slowly turned the doorknob and she entered the room. Jenna and Stacia were lounging on Jenna's bed with a laptop between them. They didn't even look up when Mo came in.

"Hey," Mo mumbled, noticing instantly how long and blond their hair was.

"Hi, Mo," Jenna replied to the computer screen. "It's about time. We didn't think you'd *ever* get here," she said dramatically. Mo stood in the doorway, awkwardly shifting her weight from one foot to the other. She set her canvas Maplewood Community Center bag on the floor. Tonight was their end-of-summer "reunion sleepover." Jenna and Stacia had gone to sleepaway camp together and then Mo had gone to Maplewood for a few weeks, so they hadn't seen each other in more than a month.

"What are you guys doing?" Mo asked. Still, neither girl had looked up at her.

"We're making a list of who is most friend-worthy for seventh grade," Stacia stated matter-of-factly.

"Huh?" asked Mo, feeling a familiar knot forming in her stomach.

"Friend-worthy," Jenna repeated emphatically. "You know, who's worthy of being in our circle of friends this year," she explained as Stacia giggled.

"This is going to be our year. We're totally going to be the most popular girls in the whole seventh grade at Emerson," Jenna explained, still staring determinedly at the computer screen.

"We would've had the sixth-grade spot last year if it hadn't been for Aubrey Dillon's *exclusive* birthday party," Stacia added, rolling onto her back to stare at the ceiling.

"Exactly," Jenna confirmed. "But now that she'll be at Bailey this year, we totally have it in the bag. Come see who we have so far," she commanded, finally looking up at Mo.

Jenna's eyes widened and she scrambled to her feet, tossing the laptop in Stacia's direction and narrowly missing her head. "No way!" she shouted. "What . . . did . . . you . . . do?!?" She stamped her feet into the carpet with each word she yelled.

Mo touched the edge of her bob yet again. "Um, it's only a haircut."

"Only a haircut?!" Stacia struggled toward the edge of the bed and was now on her feet. "You knew what our plan was, Morgan. You totally ruined it!"

"I don't see what the big deal is," Mo tried to reason, ready to tell her story. "Libby's aunt Sara needed hair models for her . . ."

"Do you think I care anything about Libby and her hillbilly aunt?" Jenna shouted.

"Excuse me?" Mo didn't think she heard that right.

"I can *not* believe you betrayed us like this. I knew

{ 7 }

you would be off doing all kinds of ridiculous country bumpkin things this summer, but I really didn't think you'd do something *this* stupid," Jenna continued, her hands planted firmly on her hips. Mo stared at her in disbelief. She couldn't help but focus on the fact that Jenna was wearing a cute new plaid sundress and matching earrings but had the most disgusted expression on her face. Mo couldn't believe how mean she looked.

She could remember when she had met Jenna and Stacia on the first day of school last year. Mo had gotten on the school bus and had found an empty seat in front of them. At first she thought the two girls were whispering and giggling about her, but just before the bus pulled in front of Wallace Emerson Middle School, Jenna had tapped Mo on the shoulder and introduced herself. The girls had offered to help Mo find her classes and had invited her to sit with them at lunch. Jenna had even given Mo one of her new fancy bracelets to wear that first day. And the rest was history. Mo had found two new BFFs on the first day of sixth grade in her strange new town and she had been determined to stick by them whatever it took.

"Yeah, Mo," Stacia picked up where Jenna left off. "I mean, look at you. You look *sooooo* small town."

Mo finally found her voice again. "I can't believe you guys," she sputtered. "You're being so nasty!"

"Nasty?" Jenna laughed. "You haven't even *seen* nasty. Hand me the laptop, Stace." Stacia leaned over the bed to retrieve the discarded computer and carefully handed it to Jenna. Jenna slammed it down on the edge of her desk.

"Number one most un-friend-worthy seventh grader at Wallace Emerson Middle School is M-O-R-G-A-N S-O-L-A-S," Jenna spelled out as she jammed her fingers into the keyboard.

"There, how's *that* for nasty?" Jenna's mouth twisted into a satisfied smirk.

"I can't believe this. It's just a haircut," Mo managed. "I just . . ."

"Well, we totally thought we could turn you into someone cool, but clearly our little project failed miserably," Jenna interrupted as Stacia giggled nervously behind her.

"What? I . . ." Mo's sneakers weighed five hundred pounds each. She tried to lift them from the carpet, but couldn't. Her mouth felt like it was full of that gross gauze they use at the dentist. She felt big tears forming in her eyes, but she still couldn't move.

"I guess it's time for you to go back to your barn now, 'cause you're definitely not staying here," Jenna half laughed at Mo and then turned toward Stacia, who nodded furiously in agreement.

Mo bent down to pick up her bag and finally felt her feet un-stick. She turned on her heel and bolted out the door, almost crashing into Jenna's mom, who was bringing a load of laundry up the stairs.

"Goodness, Morgan, slow down!"

Mo didn't slow down. She jumped the last two stairs, flung the door open, and tore across the lawn as fast as she could. Tears ran down her face just as quickly.

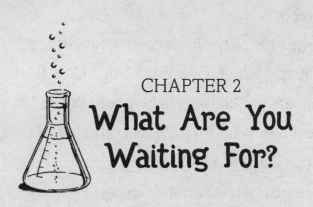

CHAPTER 2
What Are You Waiting For?

SOMEWHERE OUTSIDE MO'S SKY-BLUE comforter, Mo could hear a lawn mower starting up. Annoyed that someone would be mowing their lawn at this time of night, Mo slowly peeked her head out from under her pillow and blanket cave to check the clock.

"Geez," she said out loud, squinting at the sunlight streaming into her room. It was 11:07 A.M. "Oops," she said, laughing a little that she had thought it was still nighttime. Then, like a tidal wave washing through her room, it all flooded back to her. Standing in Jenna's bedroom, the horrible things they had said, hearing

Jenna's voice in her head. "Clearly our little project failed miserably."

Mo smashed the pillow back down over her head and breathed into it. School was starting in less than forty-eight hours and she was back where she had started a year ago: totally friendless in Kirkland. How had this happened? How had Jenna and Stacia turned out to be so mean? How had she not seen it before? Mo had always felt uncomfortable when Jenna had made fun of other girls in their sixth-grade class or when Stacia giggled at someone's outfit on the bus. She had tried to convince herself that they were just joking around and had even started to participate some of the time. But deep down, she had always known it wasn't right. Mo had been so worried about having friends in Kirkland, she had let a lot of things slide with Jenna and Stacia.

Jenna's voice came back into her head. "Number one most un-friend-worthy seventh grader." Morgan bolted upright in bed. *They're going to make fun of me at school! They're going to humiliate me and tease me in front of everyone!* If yesterday's fight was any indication, Mo knew what Jenna and Stacia were capable of.

Mo jumped up and dashed for her closet, tripping over the canvas bag she had dropped in the center of the room when she had gotten home the night before. She had run all the way from Jenna's front door to her own, gone straight to her room, gotten in bed, and had stayed there. She had cried for a long time — long enough to cry herself to sleep. She hadn't even changed into her pajamas or brushed her teeth. In fact, she was pretty sure that no one in her family even knew she had come home. She had heard her parents in the living room watching TV when she charged through the front door. She thought her mom had said, "Hi, Jeremy," thinking Mo was her older brother coming home, but Mo hadn't even bothered to correct her.

Mo hoisted herself up from the floor and flung the bag onto her desk chair. She continued to the closet and lifted a box off the shelf. She sifted through her school reports, birthday cards, and letters from Libby, and finally found last year's school yearbook.

Mo sat on the edge of her bed and opened the Wallace Emerson Middle School yearbook. "There have to be tons of potential friends I'm just forgetting about," she reassured herself.

She started flipping pages and scanning names. She saw a few faces she recognized, but hardly anyone she really knew. With each turn of a page, her confidence seeped out her toes. It was replaced with absolute dread. This was going to be a lot harder than she thought. Mo set the book on her bed and decided she'd go downstairs and get some breakfast to take her mind off things. She looked down at her green T-shirt and jean shorts from the day before and shrugged. *Why bother?* She slipped on her favorite pair of flip-flops and headed to the kitchen.

As soon as Mo reached the bottom of the stairs, she could hear what sounded like the voices of at least a hundred girls coming from the kitchen. She approached cautiously and peeked in. She had forgotten about Alexa's slumber party.

Mo's younger sister, Alexa, had had her own

end-of-summer sleepover that weekend, too, only hers had included ten girls. And Mo knew that Alexa had had a hard time narrowing down her guest list to a mere ten. She had heard Alexa begging their mom to let her invite at least two more friends.

"But, Mom, I can't invite Emily and not invite Alli, but if I don't invite Emily, she'll tell Kara not to come," Alexa had lamented earlier that week.

"I'm sorry, honey, but that is just too many girls. I have no idea where everyone is going to sleep as it is," Mrs. Solas had argued.

"But we're not going to sleep, so that's not a problem!" Alexa had responded.

Mo was totally amazed by Alexa. Her experience in Kirkland had been completely opposite of Mo's. While Alexa had always had a couple of close friends in Maplewood, now she had become the most popular almost–fourth grader in Kirkland Elementary. Mo had always thought her little sister would be begging to hang out with Mo and her friends, wanting advice and borrowing her clothes. Mo had looked forward to being annoyed by her constant presence and demands for attention. But the truth was, Mo rarely saw her. Alexa had so many activities and plans and friends, she was hardly ever home. Mo found herself secretly wishing that *she* could hang out with *Alexa*!

Mo gathered her strength and entered the kitchen. Nine-year-old girls were everywhere — giggling, screeching, and talking at full volume. In the center of it all was Alexa. She was clearly the leader of this pack.

"Hey, Alexa, do you want to be partners if we have to do a project in school?" one girl asked hopefully.

"I was going to ask her that!" Another girl pouted.

"Don't worry, guys, I'm sure there will be plenty of stuff we'll need partners for. We can switch off," Alexa assured them.

Mo shook her head. *I can't believe my little sister has an entourage,* she thought as she grabbed a banana from the fruit bowl and hurried out the sliding glass door to the backyard. *I'm an invisible loser with no friends and my* little *sister has more friends than she knows what to do with.* Mo peeled her banana with the enthusiasm of someone about to have a cavity filled. She slumped down on the bench of the picnic table and realized she wasn't alone. Jeremy and his girlfriend, Natalie, were playing catch with a football in the yard. Mo had less than nothing in common with Jeremy. He was three years older and going into tenth grade at Waverly High School. He was already on his way to becoming a star player on the football team and didn't seem to talk or think about much else. Natalie, on the other hand, was really sweet and always took time to talk to Mo. Mo sometimes wished Natalie was her older sibling instead of Jeremy. She could certainly use some advice from an older sister now.

"Hey, Mo," Natalie said as she walked up to the picnic table, twirling the football around in her hands.

"Hi," Mo replied with her mouth full of banana.

"Are you excited for seventh grade to start?" Natalie asked, pushing her long red hair out of her face.

"Uh . . . I guess so," Mo barely responded, wondering if she should confide in Natalie about her friendless dilemma.

"I *loooovvved* seventh grade," Natalie gushed. "It was such a fun year. So many fun activities and stuff to do with friends," she continued. "I had more friends in seventh grade than any other year."

Mo's shoulders slumped down. She decided now wasn't the time to mention that she might not have *any* friends in seventh grade.

"Come on, Nat, throw me the ball!" Jeremy called impatiently from across the yard.

"Guess you better go," Mo said as she stood up from the table, glad for an excuse to escape before Natalie started telling her more about her fabulous seventh-grade experience.

"Yeah, guess so," Natalie laughed. "See ya later."

Mo sneaked past Alexa and her adoring fans and decided to try the office upstairs. *Hopefully, Mom and Dad are gardening or went to the store or something,* she thought.

She opened the office door and found her parents hunched over the computer, looking at some sort of spreadsheet. Mo's parents were incredibly efficient.

They had each of their three children exactly three years apart ("three is a good, solid number," Mo's mom always said). They had run their apple orchard in Maplewood without a hitch until just after Mo's eleventh birthday last summer. Then Mo and her family had moved to Kirkland — a much bigger town, a city almost, about four hours away. Mo's grandmother had been sick and needed to move into an assisted living facility, so Mo's parents decided to sell the orchard and move to Kirkland to start a new business and be near her. Mo still didn't understand exactly what the new business was, but they called it a "consulting firm."

"Basically," Mo's dad had explained during a family meeting, "we're going to help people organize their businesses and their lives." They'd spent the last year planning and getting ready and now they were just a few weeks away from launching the business. Mo had quietly hoped that they would change their minds and try to buy back the apple orchard and move back to Maplewood, but they hadn't.

"Hi, honey." Mo's mom finally realized she was

standing there. "You're home early from Jenna's. Did you girls have fun?"

"Uh . . . it was . . . all right." Mo didn't know if she should tell them she'd been home since 8:24 the night before.

"Good, good," Mo's mom said distractedly.

"Would you mind closing the door, Mo?" Mr. Solas asked, shaking his head. "I don't know which one of those girls has that high-pitched laugh, but I don't think I can take much more of it."

"Sure, I was just going to grab the laptop." Mo picked up her mom's old laptop that she shared with Alexa and closed the office door with a quiet click.

Back in her room, Mo pushed aside a mound of clothes on the floor and sat down with her back against the side of her bed. She grabbed a light blue pillow with red stripes and propped it behind her back, and a pale red pillow with blue polka dots to put on her lap under the computer. Everything in Mo's room was coordinated in shades of blue and red. That was one thing about last summer's move that she had actually liked. She had gotten to do up her new room any way she wanted. Mo and her dad had painted the walls a pretty robin's egg blue, and Mo's mom had helped her sew a pair of airy reddish-pink curtains for her windows. She painted her bookcase a bright shade of red and found a blue desk chair at a flea market. Mo had put some framed pictures of her and Libby above her desk and a black-and-white poster of the Eiffel Tower above her bed. She couldn't wait to travel the world when she got older — Paris would be her first stop.

While she waited for the laptop to power up, Mo started thinking about the fight with Jenna and Stacia again. She felt a dry lump form in the back of her throat. *How could they have turned out to be so horrible?* she wondered. Mo had been trying to put Jenna's comment about being "a project" out of her mind, but it was impossible not to think about it. Had Jenna and Stacia ever been real friends to Mo or had they always thought of her as some sort of challenge, like a makeover show or something? Mo swallowed hard, but the lump wouldn't go away. She opened a Web page and typed in the address of Wallace Emerson Middle School. Not sure what else to do, Mo decided to look around on the school Web site and see if she could come up with some sort of friend-meeting plan.

She read the announcements on the home page. Most of them were for teachers and parents. Then she clicked on the "About" section and started reading the history of the school. "Yeah, that's not gonna help," she said aloud. Then she clicked on the "Teams" link and a big banner popped up announcing upcoming cheerleading tryouts. Mo briefly considered that option but quickly decided that she was too clumsy and awkward. Besides, she didn't know if she could keep up that level of pep all the time. She was about to click to another section on the site when the cheerleading banner caught her eye. It said: "What are you waiting for? Be the girl you always wanted to be!" Mo stared hard at the screen.

"That's it!" she said out loud. This was the perfect opportunity for Mo to step out of her comfort zone and meet new friends. After all, look where staying in her comfort zone had gotten her last year. She had spent an entire school year hanging out with two girls who actually turned out to be evil ghouls. It was time for Mo to start to feel at home in Kirkland. It was pretty clear that her parents weren't going anywhere, and Alexa and Jeremy were totally at home here. Mo was the only one who hadn't found her place.

Slowly, a plan started to form in Mo's mind. She would have her own tryouts! She would "try out" different groups at school until she found the one that fit. Even though she barely recognized most of her classmates from last year's yearbook, she was bound to find people she clicked with. Her seventh-grade class at Wallace Emerson was bigger than her whole elementary school had been in Maplewood. Surely there were tons of potential friends whom she'd just overlooked last year when she had been so busy wasting time with Jenna and Stacia. Right then and there, Mo decided that each day for the first week of school she'd pick a new group to hang out with. If a group fit, then she'd stay put, but if they didn't, then she'd try a new group the next day until she found the right one. It would be like that speed-dating show on TV or like an experiment. She would be a friendship scientist.

A pebble of excitement started building in Mo's head. This was a perfect plan. She could meet a lot of classmates in a short amount of time and be on her way to making Kirkland her home at last. She was ready to feel confident again and to "be the Mo she always wanted to be." Mo smiled. She would show Jenna and Stacia just how "friend-worthy" she could be.

Mo's mom stuck her head in the doorway to Mo's bedroom. "I need to run downtown. Wanna go get some school supplies and stuff?" she asked.

"Yes!" Mo replied enthusiastically as she jumped up from the floor. "I'm ready!"

CHAPTER 3
War and Peace

THE REST OF THE WEEKEND flew by in a blur. Mo tried to relax and enjoy the last days of her vacation and not think about school or her fight with Jenna and Stacia too much. Sunday was a beautiful day and she and Alexa had spent the afternoon at the lake with their dad. It was a great way to end the summer. She walked into the kitchen on Monday morning feeling totally prepared. *Seventh grade is going to be great!* she had chanted to herself as she got ready for school.

Alexa was in the kitchen and already talking on the phone. It sounded like she was trying to calm down someone who was having a first-day-of-school-outfit freak-out. "Why don't you just wear the jean skirt with that shirt?" Alexa asked her friend. "No, those don't go together," she replied again. "Well, what's Jenny wearing?"

Mo rolled her eyes and reached for her favorite cereal. Just then Jeremy snatched the box off the table and poured the rest into his bowl. Mo sighed as loudly as she could and glanced around for another box. Surely her mom had bought more than one. She grabbed another cereal box from the counter and started to open the top when she noticed that this one was Double Bran Morning.

"Uh, thanks, Jeremy," Mo said sarcastically.

"Huh?" he replied. Mo was pretty sure that was the only thing he had said to her all summer.

Mo glared hard at Jeremy while he wolfed down the rest of *her* cereal, but he didn't seem to notice. He was peering through his shaggy brown hair to read an article in the Kirkland paper about this year's Waverly High football team. She pushed a piece of toast into the toaster and listened to Alexa, who was still giving outfit advice to two girls (was she on a conference call?).

"Don't worry, Alli, I'm sure you look cute, too," she was saying as Mo spread jam on her toast. Mo studied Alexa's outfit as she spoke. Alexa wore a pair of dark blue corduroy pants with a blue-and-white-striped belt and a white T-shirt with a scalloped neckline and puffy sleeves. *She even dresses better than me!* Mo thought. *How is that possible?* She looked down at her own drab skirt and brown long-sleeved shirt, which already had jam spilled down the front.

Once she was off the phone, Alexa also grabbed for the cereal box but, realizing it was empty, just shrugged and plucked a granola bar from the cupboard before heading back to her room. *Unbelievable.* Mo shook her head. *She must be a robot or something . . . or maybe she's adopted. I should ask Mom.*

Mo dashed back up to her room to change her shirt and find a pair of earrings to liven up her outfit before going to meet the bus.

As Mo stood at the bus stop, a feeling came over her

that was all too familiar. That first-day-of-school feeling from last year — facing the unknown, feeling lonely, wishing Libby was there. But this time, Mo realized that when the door of the bus opened, instead of a sea of strangers, Mo would face two girls who probably planned to make her seventh-grade life totally miserable!

The bus pulled up, the door screeched open, and Mo stood in front of it like a zombie.

"Well, are you comin' or not?" the driver asked, a little annoyed.

Mo climbed the steps, her heart pumping wildly in her chest as she scanned the crowded rows. Her eyes found Jenna and Stacia instantly — sitting in their usual spot, giggling and whispering as always. Mo's stomach lurched when she realized the only empty seat was the one in front of theirs. Just like last year. The bus rolled forward and pitched Mo toward them. She felt sick and clammy and wanted to be back in her comforter and pillow cave.

As soon as Mo sat down and pretended to be busy

arranging her backpack, Jenna and Stacia's whispers and giggles became much louder.

"You know, Stacia, you are such a true friend," Jenna said to the back of Mo's head.

"So are you, Jenna. I mean, it's just so hard to find *real* friends these days," Stacia giggled.

"You're telling me," Jenna responded. "Especially ones who aren't small-town freaks with bad haircuts." The two girls launched into a new fit of laughter.

"Can you even imagine growing up in some little farm town?" Jenna continued. "You'd probably smell like cow manure, like, *all the time*."

Mo refused to cry. That wasn't part of her "be the best Mo" plan and she wasn't going to let them ruin it. Still, she couldn't believe how vicious Jenna and Stacia were being. They talked about Mo all the way to school. Their comments got nastier by the block. How had she never realized what mean girls they were? *The Mean Ghouls*, Mo decided silently. *That's their new name.*

By the time they pulled into the Emerson parking lot, Mo's eyes were full of tears. She rushed off the bus, accidentally knocking a sixth grader out of the way to put some distance between herself and the Mean Ghouls. She dodged in and out of several groups of students as she tried to make it to the front door without letting a tear slide down her cheek.

"Hey, Mo, wait up!" she heard from somewhere behind her. Joey emerged from the crowd. Mo quickly wiped at her eye and straightened her skirt.

"You are some fast walker!" Joey laughed. "You flew off the bus and then you were gone."

Mo had been so focused on Jenna and Stacia, she hadn't even seen Joey on the bus.

"Oh, sorry — yeah, I guess I am kind of fast. . . ." Mo said, feeling embarrassed.

Joey pushed open the door and Mo glanced behind her, quickly noticing Jenna and Stacia sending icy glares her way. She smiled and said, "Thanks!" to Joey. Maybe her day wasn't going to be so bad after all.

Joey walked with Mo to the office to get their locker assignments. They compared numbers and found that they were at opposite ends of the hall.

"Well, good luck today!" Joey said as he turned toward his end.

"Thanks," Mo replied. "I think I'm gonna need it."

It took Mo at least five tries to get her locker open and she was almost late for homeroom. The classroom was totally full when she arrived. She stood at the front of the room, trying desperately to find someone she recognized. Luckily, neither Stacia nor Jenna was in her homeroom class. Mo let out a small laugh of relief. It was hard to believe that just a few days ago she would have freaked out if she'd known they wouldn't be in the same homeroom.

Toward the back of the room, Mo spotted a girl whom she vaguely recognized from last year. She was even smiling at her! Mo straightened herself up and started toward her when the homeroom teacher, Mrs. Lawrence, announced, "All right, class, we have a seating chart for homeroom, so don't get too comfortable." Mo stopped in her tracks as Mrs. Lawrence began reading out the alphabetical seating arrangements and pointing to desks. Mo was assigned a seat near the door behind Annette Simon — a small girl with soft brown eyes and bold pink–framed glasses. Mo realized she remembered Annette from last year. She had won a science award and had been the best student in Mo's sixth-grade math class. She had earned the name Brainette Simon from Charlie Denis.

Mo smiled at Annette and took her seat.

"Hi, I'm Mo." *Here we go!* Mo thought to herself. Her friendship experiment was on.

"Yes, I know," Annette replied.

"Oh, I wasn't sure if . . ." Mo's confidence deflated a little.

"Aren't you friends with Jenna Halstrom and Stacia Rogers?" Annette asked, somewhat cautiously.

"No, actually," Mo replied, sliding down in her seat. "I mean, I was, but I'm not really anymore."

"Oh," Annette responded, turning more in her chair so she could face Mo. "Well, I'm Annette Simon."

"Hi, Annette." Mo smiled again.

"So." Annette now leaned onto Mo's desk with a

much friendlier look on her face. "What's your favorite subject?"

"Uh, history and English, I guess," Mo responded. "I'm not so great at science and math — all those equations and formulas and stuff aren't really my thing."

"Oh!" Annette's eyes lit up. "Well, I can totally help you with that. I mean, if you want me to. I love science and math — they're definitely my favorites."

"Yeah?" Mo asked.

"A few of my friends and I are going to start a homework club during study hall," Annette continued. "You should join us!"

"Really? That would be great!" Mo smiled back. This was going much better now! Getting in with Annette and her brainiac crowd could be really good for Mo's homework situation. She definitely needed some improvement.

"Totally. And we have a book club once a week after school, too." Annette was getting more excited as she talked. "It's really fun and we take turns bringing snacks and stuff. We're always looking for new members."

"That sounds awesome," Mo replied. She always meant to read more books, too.

Mrs. Lawrence quieted the class for morning announcements and then the bell for first period rang, signaling the official start of Mo's seventh-grade year.

"Find me at lunch and you can meet my friends," Annette said as she gathered up her things.

"OK." Mo was beaming. "See you then!"

Mo sailed through her first-period math class, smiling at everyone and trying hard to take notice of other new potential friends. Again, she was happy to discover that neither Jenna nor Stacia were in that class either. *One class down, five to go,* Mo thought to herself. There was a bigger chance of running into the Mean Ghouls with all the switching around, but Mo was relieved she had avoided them so far.

Second period was English and Mo could not believe

her luck when neither girl appeared there either. *Things are looking up!* Mo thought with a smile, but then she looked down and realized her new pen had leaked all over her skirt.

When the bell rang again, Mo hustled to the girls' bathroom to try to get some of the pen off her skirt. She rounded the corner in the bathroom and there they were. The Mean Ghouls were huddled around one of the sinks. They were digging through Jenna's giant bag of makeup. It took Mo a moment to realize that Jenna and Stacia were not alone. She'd already been replaced! Standing directly behind them was Gabby Hunter, a kind of plain-looking girl who had been in Mo's gym class last year. Mo couldn't remember her saying a single word all year long. Mo was quick to notice that Gabby's dark blond hair hung conveniently just below her shoulders. And it looked like Jenna had already given Gabby one of her bangle bracelets to wear. Now she handed Gabby a palette of eye shadow to put on. *She's their next project!* Mo realized.

"Oh, look who it is, Stace," Jenna said in a grating voice as she continued to paw through her bag. Jenna wore another new dress with a wide matching belt cinching the waist.

"Oh, great," Stacia answered. "Now the whole bathroom's going to smell like manure." Stacia wore a pair of leggings and a long striped shirt. Mo couldn't believe how much older they looked. Clearly they were trying hard to look the part of the most popular girls in seventh grade. Gabby snorted nervously as she tried to apply the eye shadow. It was clear she had never done it before and was quickly making a mess of her eyes.

"We can do this later, Gabby," Jenna said as she zipped up her bag. "Let's get out of here before we start to smell like farm animals."

Jenna and Stacia marched past Mo, and Jenna deliberately gave her a little shove toward the garbage bin.

"Yeah, let's get out of here," Gabby replied a little late. "I mean, look at that haircut, too," she said in a rehearsed-sounding way.

Mo sighed and grabbed some paper towels from the dispenser, wet them under the faucet, and tried to dab at the stain on her skirt. But all that happened was a ring of water formed around the ink stain. She turned her skirt slightly to the right, hoping that might hide the stain a bit, and looked in the mirror. Her eyes were filling with tears again, but she took a deep breath and walked toward history class. She couldn't believe the Mean Ghouls had already found a new recruit. She just had to ignore them and their dumb small-town comments and get on with finding real friends. Avoiding their jabs was going to be harder than she thought, though.

Mo's heartbeat sped up as she walked toward the lunchroom after history class. *All I have to do is find Annette, and fast,* she coached herself. Mo gripped her lunch bag tighter as she passed through the cafeteria doorway. Her eyes fell on Annette's table instantly. She was smack-dab in the center of the room at a table crowded with other students. *That's definitely them,* Mo laughed to herself. Annette was in the middle of everyone, talking excitedly and gesturing widely with her hands. All around her were very studious-looking seventh graders. They all had huge backpacks full of books resting at their feet. Several even had glasses on that just screamed "brainiac."

Mo beelined for their table before she could chicken out.

"Hey, Mo." Annette smiled up brightly at her. "Come on over."

"OK, thanks," Mo replied quietly.

"Everyone, this is Mo," Annette said in a formal voice. "Mo, this is . . . well, everyone." A few of the brainiacs nodded silently in Mo's direction and a few managed a quick "hi" before going back to their books or papers or sandwiches.

"So," started Annette, "we were just discussing which book should be our first book club discussion book this year."

"Oh, great!" replied Mo, a little too enthusiastically.

"Yeah, do you have any suggestions?" asked the boy on Mo's left as he glanced down at Mo's much smaller, fairly empty backpack.

"Um . . ." Mo had not expected to be put on the spot like this. She loved reading and she and Libby had often traded their favorite books back and forth, but this was a lot of pressure. "What about *A Wrinkle in Time*?" she finally suggested.

Mo heard a quick snicker at the end of the table and one girl covered her mouth to hide her laugh. *I guess that was the wrong answer,* Mo thought, feeling her face heat up.

"We, um, read that book two years ago for book club," Annette explained with an understanding smile. "We were actually thinking something more like *War and Peace* or *Crime and Punishment* for our intro book this year."

"Oh, OK," Mo mumbled, her eyes wide. She knew *A Wrinkle in Time* wasn't the most challenging book on the planet, but she thought an after-school book club was supposed to be for fun, not for punishment. Unsure how to rejoin the conversation, Mo decided to focus serious attention on unwrapping her sandwich instead.

The rest of the table turned their gaze back to Annette to continue the debate over *War and Peace* and *Crime and Punishment.* Mo listened quietly and took tiny bites of her sandwich that she then chewed as slowly as possible to make it appear that eating her lunch was taking all her concentration so she really couldn't participate in the conversation. Mo's eyes wandered to the corner of the lunchroom by the side door, and sure enough, there were Jenna and Stacia, and now Gabby, at *her* old lunch table. The three girls were huddled together laughing hysterically at something on a piece of paper. For a second, Mo felt a twinge of jealousy and wished that she was back in with Jenna and Stacia, laughing and joking, and *not* talking about books she thought only professors in college read for fun. She tried to shake off the feeling and turned her attention back to the conversation at her new table. The brainiacs had moved on to discussing a petition they had been working on to request that the school board add a physics class for seventh graders. Then they began to debate the inadequacies of Emerson's foreign language program.

"I mean, everybody says that Latin is dead, but that is precisely the problem!" a girl with huge, dark brown eyes and huge, dark brown hair to match was shouting from the end of the table.

Mo now fully realized that she was way out of her league at the brainiac table (not to mention, way bored). She also decided that maybe she was choosing the wrong strategy by eating slowly, so she started gulping down her sandwich to try to get away from them more quickly. They had all but forgotten she was there, though, until she started to choke on her food. All eyes turned to Mo as she sputtered ham and cheese into her napkin.

"You OK?" Annette's soft eyes looked concerned.

"I better go" was all Mo could think to say. She jumped up from the table, picked a piece of ham off her shirt, and dropped the rest of her lunch into her bag.

"See ya," she said over her shoulder to Annette as

she sprinted toward a side door, forgetting who she would be passing on her way. As she neared their table, the girls were still laughing at whatever it was on the piece of paper in front of them.

"Well, speak of the devil," Stacia blurted out, slapping her hand down on the table.

"Oh, hey, Mo," Jenna smirked. "Maybe you can help us out here. We weren't sure if we got all the details right." Jenna gestured to the drawing in front of her. It was a bad stick figure drawing of a person milking a cow. In case there was any doubt the person was supposed to be Mo, they had written "MORGAN" and an arrow pointing to the figure.

"That's so original," Mo responded, her voice a little shaky. "You guys really have nothing better to do?" Mo dropped her lunch bag in the trash and hurried out of the cafeteria before the Mean Ghouls could make another nasty comment.

CHAPTER 4
Drumming for Dummies

THAT EVENING AFTER DINNER, Mo grabbed the cordless phone from her parents' office and hustled to her room. She had been dying to talk to Libby all day and she knew she'd better take the opportunity now before Alexa started bugging her for the phone. She was probably the only seventh grader in all of Kirkland that didn't have a cell phone. She had been begging her parents since last year to get her one — especially because Jenna and Stacia had made such a big deal about how *annoying* it was that Mo didn't have one. But Mr. and Mrs. Solas had held firm and told Mo they would reconsider once her grades were in at the end of the semester.

"Lib, hey, it's Mo."

"Hi! I was hoping you'd call me!" Libby responded enthusiastically. "How was it today? How was being back and everything?"

Mo had avoided Libby all weekend, so Libby had no idea about the falling-out between Mo and Jenna and Stacia.

Mo dove backward onto her bed. "Ugh, Libby, everything's terrible. I went to Jenna's on Friday for a sleepover and it was a huge disaster! They totally freaked out about my haircut and they said I was small town and just a project," Mo blurted out all in one breath.

Before Libby had answered the phone, Mo wasn't sure what she was going to say. In a way, she felt dumb about the situation with Jenna and Stacia — like she should have known better than to be friends with girls like that in the first place. She didn't want Libby to think that she had become like them or something.

"Wait, what happened?" Libby asked, confused. "They said you were a *project*?"

"Uh-huh," Mo responded quietly. "Like they had never really been friends with me, like they just thought they could turn me into a cool girl instead of a . . . what did they call me? Oh, yeah, a country bumpkin."

"Mo, that's ridiculous!" Libby shouted into the phone. "I can't believe they said that to you. I thought they were your closest friends there!"

"Yeah, well, I guess I have pretty bad friendship skills in Kirkland."

"It's totally not your fault, Mo," Libby reassured her. "I can't imagine what it feels like to go to a new school. I thought you were so brave last year, starting middle school in a totally new place and everything."

"Not brave enough to avoid the Mean Ghouls, apparently," Mo half laughed. "So, tell me about your day." Mo didn't want to think about Jenna and Stacia anymore.

"Oh, it was . . . fine." Mo could tell Libby was trying to play down her day.

"No, tell me, I really want to know. How are Max and Caroline and Sasha?"

"They're good!" Libby replied, perking up. "We all had four classes together so that was fun and Mr. Hawthorne let us sit outside for English and Tony Arroyo got in trouble for falling asleep under a tree and missing geometry." She laughed.

Mo let out a small noise that was supposed to be a laugh for Libby's benefit, but it sounded more like a sick kitten.

"Mo, I'm sorry," Libby sighed. "I feel bad talking about everyone since things are . . . since you're having a hard time there."

"No, it's OK, I just miss you guys." Mo's throat tightened against the tears that were building up.

"I know you'll find good friends there," Libby continued. "Maybe you just haven't met the right ones yet."

Just then the phone clicked and beeped as someone began to dial a new number.

"Hello?" Mo and Libby asked in unison.

"Hello," Alexa replied.

"Alexa, I'm on the phone!" Mo said loudly into the receiver.

"Oh, I wondered where the cordless was," she replied. "Well, I need to make a call. It's really, um, important."

Mo sighed. "Get off the line and I'll tell you when I'm done."

"Well, hurry up, Mo, it's an emergency," Alexa whined.

"The sooner you hang up, the sooner I'll be done, Alexa!" Mo argued.

"Fine . . . hurry," Alexa added before hanging up.

Libby laughed. "Some things haven't changed, huh?"

"I think I'm starting to wish my parents would just get Alexa a cell phone instead of me!" Mo laughed back.

"Well, unfortunately, I have to go do my homework anyway. I can't believe how much I have already," Libby replied.

There was a long pause on the line.

"Are you going to be OK, Mo?"

"Yeah." Mo sighed, letting her throat relax a little bit. "I'm working on a little experiment."

"What kind of experiment?" Libby asked.

"A friendship experiment," Mo responded. "I'll keep you posted on my results."

"Uh, all right." Libby sounded hesitant about hanging up. "I know it will work out."

"Yeah, me, too," Mo responded. "Bye, Lib."

"At least I hope it will," Mo said to herself after clicking the phone off.

The next morning as Mo waited for the bus, she tried to visualize the seats in her head. She was determined to sit as far away from Jenna and Stacia as possible — even if it meant sitting in the bus driver's lap! When the bus pulled up, Mo got on and focused her attention on the front section of seats. Her eyes locked on Joey listening to his iPod and sitting alone three seats back from the driver. She rushed toward his seat and then hesitated, but as soon as he saw her, he grinned and moved his backpack to the floor.

"Hey there," he said as he removed his earphones.

"Hi, are you sure you don't mind if I sit here?" Mo's voice squeaked a little.

"Sure, not at all." Joey smiled again.

As Mo slid into the seat, she glanced back toward the Mean Ghouls and saw their horrified faces out of the corner of her eye.

"So I haven't really seen you hanging out with Jenna lately," Joey commented. "What's up with that?"

"Well, we had sort of, um, a falling-out, I guess." Mo wasn't sure how much to say about the situation. Jenna was Joey's twin sister, after all. She didn't want to be too mean about things.

"That sucks," Joey replied. "It was fun having you around."

Mo smiled in spite of herself and felt her cheeks flush. "Yeah, you probably won't be seeing too much of me around your house anymore," she said. "But you know, there's school and stuff," she rushed to add, but then felt embarrassed.

"Yeah, definitely," Joey responded.

Mo and Joey talked all the way to school. They talked about their teachers and classes, and Joey described a silly fight he had had with Jenna the night before. Mo had never realized how funny and easy to talk to he was. Whenever he used to come to Jenna's room to ask a question or to sit and watch TV with them, Jenna would shout at him to go away. Jenna's mom had been just as quick to tell him to "stop bugging the girls."

When the bus pulled in front of Wallace Emerson, Jenna and Stacia clawed their way to the front and stood over Mo and Joey's seat.

"I don't know what you think you're doing sitting with my brother, Morgan, but you better be careful what you say," Jenna hissed in Mo's face.

"Whoa, what's your problem?" Joey looked shocked.

"Mind your own business, Joey!" Jenna hissed at him. "Just stick to your little do-gooder projects and stay away from *her*!" she added and then stalked off the bus. Stacia struggled to keep up with her while glaring back at them.

"What the heck was that?" Joey was truly stunned.

"Well, like I said, we had a bit of a falling-out." Mo couldn't help but laugh a little.

"Falling-out? More like total destruction!" Joey replied.

They walked toward the school not saying too much. Mo could tell that Joey wasn't quite over what had just happened. And she wondered what Jenna had meant by "do-gooder projects." That was a weird thing to say.

"I knew my sister wasn't exactly the nicest kid on the block, but I didn't know she was being like *that*," Joey said, staring blankly ahead.

"Sorry, Joey, I'm sure your sister's not always as mean as she seems. . . ." Mo trailed off, knowing now that it wasn't true.

Joey opened his mouth to speak but was interrupted by the first bell. "Yeah, well, anyway, see ya later," he said quietly and turned toward his locker at the opposite end of the hall.

"OK, bye," Mo said awkwardly, watching Joey walk in the other direction. *Is he mad at me, too, now?* she thought, totally confused. *Maybe because they're twins, that automatically means he has to be on her side.* Mo turned and hurried toward her locker. Since it had taken her so many tries to open it yesterday, she didn't want to be late.

Mo knew that Annette Simon would be waiting in homeroom and she wasn't sure what to do. She also knew that the brainiacs were not her newfound BFFs. But she really liked Annette and didn't want to hurt her feelings. She slumped into her seat behind Annette, who was already scribbling furious notes in her science lab journal.

Maybe she won't even realize I'm here, Mo hoped silently, just as Annette put down her pencil and swiveled in her seat.

"Hey, Mo, I wanted to apologize for lunch yesterday," Annette said softly.

"For what?" Mo was surprised. "I was going to apologize to you for leaving so quickly."

"I know my friends and I can be a little . . . intense. I'm sorry if we scared you off or anything," Annette continued.

"Oh, no, it's fine," Mo stuttered. "I guess I was a little thrown off by the *War and Peace* thing. You know, I don't think I'm going to have time to do a book club this year." Mo was relieved that there was no way she'd be reading that book and spending her precious after-school time talking about it!

"That's totally no big deal." Annette smiled knowingly. "But the study hall homework group still stands if you ever need help with math or science or anything. . . ."

"Really? Thanks, Annette!" Mo couldn't believe how easy that was. She was so happy that Annette's feelings weren't hurt.

"By the way," Annette whispered as Mrs. Lawrence began the morning announcements. "I meant to tell you yesterday that I really like your hair! I wanted to get mine cut like that this summer, but I was too chicken."

Mo grinned. "Well, if you need someone to go with you to do it, I'm your girl."

As Mo's lunch period grew closer that morning, she felt her stomach growing tenser. Even though things went much more smoothly with Annette than she'd thought they would, there was no way she was going to trap herself at that lunch table again to listen to them recite chemistry formulas or tell jokes in Latin. However, there was also no way she would give the Mean Ghouls the satisfaction of seeing her eat alone.

Mo took as much time as she could to get her lunch bag out of her locker — she opened and closed it three times, pretending the door was jammed. Then she dug around in her lunch bag a few times, organizing her sandwich, apple, and cookie in different order. Then she put her backpack on the floor and rearranged all her books and notebooks for her afternoon classes. By then the hall monitor had walked by twice to tell her to get to the cafeteria.

Mo had finally started walking toward the lunchroom when she heard several voices and a few instrument noises coming from the band room, just off the gym. She approached the door and saw a big poster board propped up on an easel, announcing that marching band tryouts were taking place after school that day. Mo peered in the window of the band room door and saw a group of students talking and laughing, and most important, eating their lunches. She took a deep breath, chanted "Be the best Mo you can be" to herself, and opened the door to the band room.

Mo stood awkwardly in the doorway and cleared her throat. "Um, is this where the marching band tryouts are?" she asked, trying to make her voice louder than the noise in the room.

All eyes turned in Mo's direction for a second and a few heads nodded vaguely, but most of the students continued to laugh and goof around — except for one unlikely pair, who jumped to their feet and dashed toward Mo.

"I'm Christine Marsten, second chair flute," the girl

with the light brown complexion and straight dark hair stated as she stuck out her hand.

Mo quickly shook her hand. "I'm Morgan Solas, well, Mo actually."

"And I'm Stanley Stokes, well, Stan actually, first chair trombone," said the boy, extending his stark white hand spotted with bright orange freckles.

"Nice to meet you guys," Mo managed, feeling a little overwhelmed.

"Come sit by us," Christine said, ushering Mo to the second row of band chairs.

Stan and Christine made a place for Mo between them and instantly started grilling her with questions about music while she unwrapped her peanut butter and jelly sandwich. They barely touched their own lunches, they were so eager to find out more about Mo.

"What instrument do you play?"

"How come you weren't in band last year?"

"Who's your favorite composer, Mozart or Beethoven?"

"Do you have your own piece of music for tryouts?"

"What kind of cheese do you like?" That was Stan's question and it received weird looks from both Christine and Mo.

Before Mo had even taken one bite of her sandwich, she had revealed herself to be a second-year drum player who liked Mozart and cheddar cheese.

The rest of the lunch period flew by as Stanley and Christine coached Mo on the best techniques for tryouts later that afternoon.

"Lock eyes with the band leader as often as you can," Christine suggested. "Then he'll really know how serious you are."

"And don't forget to stand up straight," she added.

"Before you give them the name of the piece you're going to do, tell them a joke," Stan offered, again receiving weird looks from the girls. "Well, only if it's a really good joke that's going to help your chances. My first year, I told a joke about a saxophone and a piano and it didn't go over very well. . . ."

"Why are you so weird, Stan?" Christine asked, slightly annoyed.

"Chris, I'm just saying!" he argued. "Geez, some people are so uptight."

Mo laughed. She liked Christine and Stanley's banter and felt relaxed around them, but what was she going to do about the actual tryouts? She had never played drums in her life! And could she really see herself drumming out school spirit songs with Christine and Stan on the football field all year?

Mo was about to tell them the truth about why she came to the band room when the bell rang.

"Shoot!" Christine exclaimed. "I have a math quiz and I left my notebook in my locker!"

"Guys, wait a sec," Mo tried to interrupt as Christine and Stanley hustled around her, gathering up their things.

"Don't be nervous, Mo," Stanley assured her. "Just meet us here after seventh period and we'll give you some more last-minute tips."

"No, I just . . ." Mo tried again.

"Yeah, I'm sure Stan will have a joke ready for you." Christine rolled her eyes. "See you after school, Mo!"

And with that, Stan and Chris shot toward the door and out of the room. Mo could still hear Christine lecturing Stan on making a better first impression and not being "so weird."

Before she knew it, Mo was standing alone in the empty band room. She spotted a drum set in the corner and started toward it, thinking maybe she'd at least give it a try, when she remembered that Stan and Christine weren't the only ones who needed to get to class!

"Right, science lab," Mo reminded herself out loud.

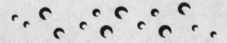

Mo got in trouble three times in science lab — twice with Ms. Clarin and once with her lab partner — for trying to drum out some sort of rhythm on the lab table.

"What are you doing, Solas?" her partner, Martin Paterson, asked impatiently.

"Sorry, nothing." Mo flushed, setting down the two plastic droppers she was holding. "What's the next step?"

During study hall, Mo got a pass to the library and rushed to find any kind of how-to book on drums. She found *Drums for Dummies* in the self-help section and settled down in the corner of the library with two pencils for drumsticks. She tried desperately to remember any techniques her brother used on that weird rock-band video game of his. She thought about music videos or parades she had seen that featured drummers. She tapped her foot and tried to create a beat on her lap with the pencils. It wasn't going very well.

There's no way I can actually go through with this, Mo thought as she walked toward the band room after the final bell. *If the Mean Ghouls found out about me doing drum tryouts, they would never let me live it down.* Mo started to run down the hall, hoping she could catch Christine and Stan before the tryouts began and tell them the truth. She arrived to find the room completely overrun with students. There were at least twice as many students as had been in the room at lunch. Christine and Stan spotted her immediately and swooped down to shuttle her into the drum line. They both talked excitedly at once.

"OK, so the drummers go last, but don't let that make you nervous," Christine coached. "Just try to tune everybody out."

"Did you bring your own piece of music?" Stanley asked.

Mo shook her head silently, feeling all the color drain from her face.

"It's OK." Stan looked a little alarmed at Mo's expression. "Don't worry, here's the sheet music for the piece that the drummers play if they don't bring their own."

Mo stared down at the jumble of notes. "Guys, I . . ." she started just as the band teacher clapped his hands and shouted for everyone to get in their appropriate lines. "Listen," Mo started again. Stan patted her on the shoulder and Christine squeezed her hand, and then they hurried to their own lines.

One by one, the other students gave their performances. Christine and Stan both played their pieces perfectly and then stood at the back of the classroom waiting excitedly for Mo's turn. The drummers were the last to audition and Mo stood fourth in the line. She couldn't believe she'd let things go this far. Why hadn't she forced Stan and Christine to listen to her?

Just before the first drummer took his spot in the front of the room, Mo took a step backward and slipped out of the line. As she did so, she watched the looks on Christine and Stan's faces slip, too. Mo tiptoed to the back of the room, aware that many students were staring at her. Stan and Christine motioned her toward the door of the band room, and they moved quickly into the hall.

"I'm really sorry, you guys," Mo finally managed to say, hiding her face in her hands. "I have never played a musical instrument in my life, well, except for piano for, like, two minutes when I was eight, but that's another story."

Stan and Christine looked hurt. "But why . . ." Christine started.

"I just saw everyone in the band room laughing and having a good time at lunch and I wanted to be a part of things, I guess," Mo explained. "I tried to tell you before tryouts started . . . but I shouldn't have even let it go on that long. I'm really sorry."

Christine finally seemed to snap out of her daze and lct out a giant laugh. That seemed to pull Stan back to reality and he began to laugh, too.

"So you've never played drums?" Christine laughed.

"Nope, never." Mo shook her head. "Come on, let's go to Mr. Pizza and I'll buy you guys a slice. I totally owe you."

"Yes, you do!" Stan and Christine agreed instantly.

Mo had a great time at Mr. Pizza with Christine and Stanley. They laughed hysterically about Mo's pale expression as she stood in the drum line. They laughed even harder when they tried to imagine what Mo's drum solo would have been like. Christine came up with a pretty good impression of how her song would have sounded. Then Stan told the girls a few of the band jokes he had stored up. And even when the Mean

Ghouls came in and made a nasty comment as they passed Mo's table, Stanley and Christine just shrugged it off and kept laughing. Mo knew she wouldn't be spending too much more time in the band room, but she also knew that she could count on Christine and Stan anytime she needed a laugh.

CHAPTER 5
Teamwork

THE NEXT MORNING, Mo found her entire family in the kitchen when she came downstairs before school. Mo's mom was even making eggs — something she didn't normally do on weekdays.

"What's the occasion?" Mo asked as she poured herself a glass of orange juice.

"Well, besides dinnertime I've barely seen you kids this week, so I just wanted to catch up and see how school was going so far," Mrs. Solas replied, shoveling scrambled eggs onto five separate plates. "Besides, your father and I are going to be a lot busier as soon as we are open for business in a couple of weeks."

"At least we hope," Mo's dad laughed.

"So give us the scoop on your week at school," Mrs. Solas continued.

"Well," Alexa chimed right in. "Alli and Emily are already in a fight, but luckily they are in different classes, so I don't have to hear about it all day."

Mr. and Mrs. Solas laughed and Jeremy shook his head.

"I really like Mr. Williams, though, and there's a new girl in my class that's super fun and me and Jenny are starting a club and, oh, yeah, can I stay at her house on Friday night, *pleeeease*?" Alexa said in one long breath.

"Probably. But we'll see, honey," Mrs. Solas said as she smiled.

"What about you, Jeremy?" Mr. Solas asked. "How's the team looking?"

"Really good," Jeremy responded, his mouth full of egg. "I think we'll make it to State this year, no problem."

"And what about your classes?" Mrs. Solas asked, shaking her spatula in Jeremy's direction.

"They're good, you know." Jeremy shrugged. "Oh, by the way, a bunch of the guys on the team are going to this big athletic store in Anderson on Saturday. It's supposed to have equipment that no stores in Kirkland have, so I was wondering if I could go with them. And then Natalie wants to go to some movie at this artsy theater somewhere on Saturday night, so I'll probably be gone all day."

"Probably. We'll see," Mrs. Solas responded again.

"And what about you, missy?" Mrs. Solas turned her attention to Mo. "How are Jenna and Stacia? I haven't even seen them since you got back from Maplewood."

"They're fine," Mo snapped. "I mean, whatever . . . it's not like they have to be hanging around all the time or something."

"Watch that attitude, Morgan," said Mr. Solas.

Mo took one more bite of her eggs and then pushed her plate away. "I have to get to school early," she mumbled and stood up from the table, ignoring the confused looks from her family.

"You haven't even finished your eggs," Mo's mom called after her.

"Sorry, Mom, gotta go," she called back.

Mo dashed up to her room, grabbed her backpack, and bounded back down the stairs. She let the front door close a little too loudly, but didn't care. She was embarrassed about the situation with Jenna and Stacia and didn't want to talk about it at breakfast with the whole family. Obviously, Alexa and Jeremy had stuff going on that they *wanted* to talk about — why couldn't everybody just focus on them and leave her alone for a while? At least until she had more time to work on her friendship experiment.

Mo stood in the front yard unsure what to do next. It was too far to walk to school and she wasn't going back in the house to ask for a ride at this point. Her only option was to stand at the bus stop and wait it out.

Mo shifted back and forth, impatiently waiting for the bus. She was about to pull one of her schoolbooks from her backpack when a tall girl with short black hair and a light coffee-colored complexion walked toward her.

"Hi," Mo said as the girl approached, taking long-legged steps toward the bus stop.

The girl glanced behind her. "Me?" she asked.

"Yes . . ." Mo started, looking a little confused. "I'm Mo."

"Yeah, I know. I'm Jordan."

Mo was even more confused. "I've never seen you on the bus before. How did you know my name?"

"My mom usually gives me a ride to school, but she had to go to work early for a meeting. I took the bus a few times last year. I remember you sitting with Jenna and Stacia. You guys made fun of my sneakers once," Jordan said matter-of-factly.

"Oh." Mo was shocked. She didn't even remember Jordan from last year but Jordan had remembered her instantly . . . as one of the Mean Ghouls.

"Yep, I definitely remember that," Jordan said again.

"Uh, I'm really sorry about that." Mo felt her face flaming up. "I'm not friends with those girls anymore. N-n-not that that's any excuse for making fun of you . . ." Mo stammered. "I just, I'm sorry."

"It's fine," Jordan responded. "I never let that kind of stuff bother me anyway. But I am glad to hear you're not hanging out with them anymore."

"Thanks," Mo replied, wishing the bus would come so she could sink into a seat and bury her head in her backpack.

"So, how's seventh grade so far?" Jordan asked.

"It's OK." Mo was surprised that Jordan still wanted to talk to her.

"Have you had gym class yet?" Jordan continued.

"No, it starts today. I have it sixth period," Mo groaned. She had never been a big fan of gym class.

"Me, too!" Jordan said excitedly. "I can't wait!"

"Really?" Mo couldn't believe anyone would be excited about gym.

"Totally. I love sports. I play basketball, run track, swim, you name it. What sports do you play?"

"Uh, none really. I mean, I play basketball in the driveway with my brother sometimes, but that's about it." Mo felt a little embarrassed by her lack of athletic ability.

"Well, basketball tryouts are coming up. You should totally go out for the team!" said Jordan enthusiastically.

An image of yesterday's marching band debacle flashed through Mo's mind. "Yeah . . . maybe."

Mo and Jordan were startled by the screeching tires of the bus as it approached their stop.

"Wanna sit together?" Mo asked hopefully.

"Sure!" Jordan flashed a smile.

They passed Joey's seat when they got on the bus, but he was busy listening to his iPod and scribbling answers to his math homework, so he didn't even notice them. They found a seat together just two rows in front of Jenna and Stacia. Mo had hoped they would get a spot farther away from them. She wondered if they would still make fun of her.

"How's your new marching band career?" Jenna asked loudly in Mo's direction.

I guess so, Mo thought.

"Yeah, I didn't know they played drums on the farm," Stacia sputtered.

Jordan looked behind her and then back at Mo. "They're talking about you, aren't they?"

"Unfortunately, yes," Mo responded sheepishly. "I'm their new target this year."

"It totally smells like manure in here now," Jenna started again. "The bus driver should make all students who smell like farm animals ride in a special section."

"Yeah, like on the roof or something," Stacia added and both girls screeched with laughter.

"What is all that farm stuff about?" Jordan asked.

"I moved here last year from Maplewood, where my family owned an apple orchard and my best friend lives on a farm," Mo explained. "I guess that's the best they can come up with."

"At least it's a little more original than bad sneakers." Jordan laughed.

Mo blushed again. "Yeah, I guess so."

"Well, my uncle owns a farm and I visit him almost every summer. I love it!" said Jordan.

Jenna started to make another loud farm comment

and Jordan turned around and responded with the loudest "*Moooooooooooo!*" Mo had ever heard. Now it was their turn to laugh.

"Thanks for your help on the bus," Mo said as the girls parted ways at the front of the school.

"Anytime." Jordan smiled. "I'll see you in sixth period, if not before, and you should definitely think about basketball tryouts!"

Mo had left her house so abruptly that morning, she hadn't taken her lunch. She dug through her backpack and luckily found a five-dollar bill she had forgotten about. Unfortunately, though, this meant she couldn't escape to the library or hide in the computer lab with her sack lunch. She'd have to face the hot lunch line and the swarming cafeteria.

Mo slid her tray along the metal lunch counter and watched a blob of spaghetti fall onto her plate. She had grabbed a juice and a roll and started toward the cashier when she bumped right into Jordan.

"Oh, hey!" Jordan greeted her happily. "Fancy meeting you here."

Mo felt a wave of relief and decided to ask Jordan to join her for lunch. She needed to keep up with her friend experiment after all. "Hey, let's sit together."

"Definitely. My table is right over there." Jordan nodded her head toward a group of girls sitting slightly to the left of Annette Simon's brainiac table.

"Oh, OK," Mo replied. She wasn't sure what she had expected. Of course Jordan had friends at lunch. Mo seemed to be the only one in the entire school who didn't have a table full of friends.

"Come on, I'll introduce you," Jordan offered as she made her way through the crowded lunchroom.

"Hey, guys, this is Mo. Mo, this is Gina, Esther, Lacey, Sharlene, and Tori." Mo and Jordan pulled extra chairs up to the table and sat down.

"So, we were just talking about basketball tryouts," Sharlene explained.

Mo's eyes wandered around the table as she choked down her school spaghetti. Mo was just as tall as the other girls, but they all seemed a lot more athletic than her. *Maybe I should start using that treadmill in the basement,* Mo thought, feeling a little wimpy. Most of the girls had sweatshirts or T-shirts with their favorite team's logo on it. They also all wore pretty serious-looking sneakers. Mo scooted her chair farther under the table so no one would notice her very nonathletic flat black shoes.

"Yeah, who do you think's gonna crash and burn during tryouts?" Esther pounded her fist into her palm and laughed.

"There's no way Elisa's going to make the team again this year. She was so *bad* last year!" Gina added.

Mo was surprised by how ultracompetitive Jordan's friends were. Jordan hadn't seemed that way on the bus.

"Did you watch the recap of last year's championship game on TV last night?" Tori chimed in. "Those girls killed it!"

Mo listened as the rest of the table continued to talk about basketball. She tried to think of some way to join the conversation but had no idea who the best WNBA players were or how Emerson's team would compare to other middle schools in Kirkland this year. Jordan smiled at Mo, seeming to sense that she didn't totally feel at home at the table. "Oops, you spilled some spaghetti," she pointed out with a giggle.

Mo looked down to see a giant blob of spaghetti sauce on her favorite blue shirt. "I guess I better go try to get this off." Mo stood up from the table. "I'll see you in gym class, OK?"

Mo hustled her tray to the disposal area and tried to cover the stain with her hand. *At least I got out of that one before someone tried to put me in a headlock or something,* she thought as she dodged past crowded tables and out into the hall.

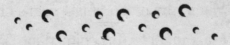

After science lab, Mo arrived in the locker room at the start of sixth period to find Jordan and her entire lunch table getting changed for gym.

In the opposite corner of the room stood Stacia and Gabby. *Great,* Mo said to herself as she walked toward the only unoccupied corner, *this is going to go well.*

Once changed and out at the edge of the baseball field, Mo stood awkwardly next to Jordan while Mr. Sanchez split the girls into two teams. Mo managed to avoid being put on the same team as Stacia and Gabby but ended up paired with Jordan, Esther, Gina, and Sharlene.

Mo's team took the field first, so she quickly retreated to the outfield, hoping to avoid too many orders from the AAs (Aggressive Athletes) — her new name for Jordan and her crew.

"Hey, aren't you Morgan?" she heard from behind her as she jogged farther into right field. Mo turned to see a girl from her homeroom class.

"Yeah, hi." Mo waited for her to catch up.

"I'm Nicole. I've hardly seen you around since yesterday in homeroom, but I wanted to say hi," she said, her big brown eyes sparkling.

"MO! HEADS UP!" Esther shouted with the lungs of an auctioneer, from the pitcher's mound. "EVERYBODY GET READY!"

"Yikes," Nicole giggled. "I'm not sure I *am* ready for this!"

"Tell me about it," Mo laughed back. "The AAs are a little intense for me."

"AAs?" asked Nicole.

"Oh, sorry — the Aggressive Athletes — I just came up with that nickname for the other girls on our team."

"That's perfect!"

Just then the bat cracked, and before they knew it, the ball was sailing directly toward them. Mo and Nicole put their gloves up ready for the ball, and it fell right between them.

"Come *on*!" Gina shouted and stamped her foot from first base. "Get it together out there!"

"Yeah, you guys," Esther screamed out. "You shoulda had that."

The two girls erupted into a fit of laughter and spent the rest of the game huddled together in the outfield talking and laughing. Mo was relieved that Nicole didn't bring up the fact that she had been friends with Jenna and Stacia. *At least somebody doesn't recognize me as one of the Mean Ghouls,* she thought.

On the way back to the locker room, Mo and Nicole continued to chat until Esther pulled Mo aside and gave her a lecture about teamwork and keeping her "eye on the ball." By the time Mo managed to free herself from Esther's rant, Nicole was gone.

As everyone filed out of the locker room for seventh period, Mo spotted Jordan and rushed over to her.

"Hey, Jordan, I just wanted to let you know that I don't think I'll be going out for the basketball team. I think Kirkland team sports are a little too . . . intense for me."

"No big deal," Jordan said with a smile. "I know my friends are a little serious about sports sometimes — I hope they didn't bother you."

"Not at all," Mo replied. She was just proud of herself for being honest with Jordan and not getting into another marching-band situation!

CHAPTER 6
Cold Lunch

THE FOLLOWING MORNING, Mo stood in her bathrobe with a knotted towel on her head, staring blindly into her closet. She had met plenty of new people during the week so far, but she had thought by now she would have found the perfect new group of friends. This friendship experiment was turning out to be harder than she expected. Mo sighed and sat down at her desk to scan the list of groups and cliques she had made the night before. Crossed off the list were the brainiacs, the band kids, and the AAs. Next on the list were the preppy kids. As Mo had exited the lunchroom with her spaghetti-stained shirt the previous afternoon, she had spotted a table of clean-cut preppy-looking students in the corner of the room near Jenna and Stacia's table. She was sure she noticed April from her English class in the bunch. *Maybe I'll try to talk to April today,* Mo thought. *I think she smiled at me in English on Monday. . . .*

Mo jumped up and dove headfirst into her closet to dig out a pair of squeaky clean Keds that she knew were hidden somewhere in the back. Then she found a light pink polo shirt crammed into a pile of T-shirts on a shelf and a brown-and-pink-plaid pleated skirt. She added a pair of brown kneesocks to the mix and nodded at herself in the mirror. She was satisfied that her look was significantly more preppy than usual.

When Mo skipped into the kitchen to grab some breakfast, the looks of her siblings almost made her change her mind.

"What?" she asked accusingly.

"Uh, nothing, it's just that you look so . . ." Alexa started.

"Preppy?" Mo finished.

"Yeah . . . something like that." Alexa was still confused. Alexa's outfit, on the other hand, was perfect again. She wore a pair of light blue capri jeans with a cream-colored shirt and brown flats. A matching brown headband held her perfectly shaped long brown hair in place.

"I'm just experimenting with my look a little, is that all right with you?" Mo snapped.

"You don't have to get mean about it, Mo," Jeremy defended Alexa. "It's true, you *never* dress like that."

"How would you know? When was the last time you even noticed my existence?" Mo asked sharply.

"Geez" was Jeremy's only response before returning to his bowl of cereal and the history book propped open in front of him.

Alexa scooted by Mo, gave her one last look, and left the kitchen. Mo's face flushed. She knew she had been snarky, but the pressure of her friendless situation was starting to wear on her. She never thought it would be this hard to make new friends in Kirkland. And the hardest part of all was that she already had the friends she wanted back in Maplewood, but she couldn't be there. She resented the fact that Alexa and Jeremy were fitting in so perfectly here — better, in fact, than they had in Maplewood. All Mo wanted was to feel confident again like she used to in her hometown.

She shook her head and grabbed an orange from the fruit bowl, then turned to get her backpack and face the morning bus ride of doom.

There was no Jordan and no Joey on the school bus — only the Mean Ghouls with their usual ugly sneers. The only good thing was that Mo found a seat farther away from theirs than normal. She had meant to bring her headphones with her this time to tune out their comments but had totally forgotten them after her uncomfortable confrontation with Jeremy and Alexa in the kitchen. She pulled her science lab journal out of her backpack and decided to reread her entry from the night before.

Suddenly, there was a commotion at the back of the

bus and Mo turned to see Jenna standing in the middle of the aisle with a notebook in her hand.

"Good morning, fellow Wallace Emerson Middle School bus riders," she stated with authority. "This morning Stacia and I would like to take a little bus poll on the way to school."

Mo slunk down in her seat. She already knew what was coming. *These girls are never going to stop!* Mo shouted inside her head. *I can't believe this is happening!*

Stacia was already giggling uncontrollably and nervously twisting her hair around her finger while Jenna spoke. "How many of you would like to see farm kids banned from attending Wallace Emerson?"

At first hardly anyone was paying attention to Jenna, except for two sixth-grade boys who seemed like they'd say or do anything she wanted them to.

"Come on now, people," Jenna continued even louder. "Don't you think farm kids should have to attend their own school? We don't need their small-town ways and simple-life ideas corrupting our educations, do we?" She was shouting now.

"Hey, you, in the back!" the bus driver called, glaring into the rearview mirror. "Sit down and be quiet!"

Jenna ignored the driver and continued with her poll. "I mean, just imagine what would happen if we let a bunch of hillbillies tell us what to do?"

Now it seemed like a few more kids were listening, because the laughter on the bus was growing louder and louder.

"So, all those in favor of banning farm kids from Wallace Emerson, raise your hand."

Most of the sixth grade hands were in the air, but when Jenna yelled, "RAISE YOUR HAND" a few more times, several other hands hovered lazily as well.

"Don't make me stop this bus, young lady!" the driver finally threatened.

Jenna sat down with a satisfied smirk. "I'm done now anyway. It's clear no one wants hillbillies at our school and MORGAN SOLAS will be the first to go." Jenna pointed her perfectly polished fingernail at Mo and shook it wildly to make sure everyone could see exactly who she was referring to.

Mo was at the front door of the bus before the driver had even pulled into the parking lot.

"What is with you kids today?" the bus driver asked, clearly out of patience.

"Sorry," Mo mumbled, fighting back tears. "I just need to . . ." She didn't even finish before running off the bus and into the school.

Mo ran in the opposite direction of her locker, toward the girls' bathroom. She was just about to turn a sharp right into the doorway when she practically collided with Joey.

"Whoa, there you go again, moving at the speed of light!" Joey laughed and steadied his armload of books. "You OK?" he asked as he focused on Mo's face.

"Um, just a rough morning, I guess," Mo said quietly to her shoes, hoping Joey wouldn't see the tears about to spill from her eyes.

Just then a sixth-grade boy from Mo's bus walked by and let out a long, slow *"Moooooo"* in her direction.

"Let me guess — Jenna, right?" Joey said angrily. "I had to come in early to help with a volunteer project," he continued. "Somehow I knew she would do something mean if I wasn't on the bus."

"It's not your fault." Mo finally looked up at Joey. "Really, I'm OK." The last thing Mo wanted was for Joey to confront Jenna. Then she'd know for sure just how bothered Mo was by all the teasing. "I better get to my locker," Mo said, trying to perk up. "I'll see you later."

Mo spent most of math class trying to decide whether or not to call her mom and tell her she was sick. Every time Mo started to feel an ounce better about her situation, Jenna's comments from the bus popped into her mind to make her feel miserable again. By the end of class, though, Mo had convinced herself that she had to continue with her experiment. She would never find the friends she wanted to have if she let the Mean Ghouls get to her. English class was next and Mo was going to talk to April. Mo straightened her posture as she walked toward her English room. She shook her short brown bob as if hoping the insults would fall from her head.

After the bell, Mo's English teacher, Ms. Vaughn, asked the class to choose partners for a vocabulary exercise.

Perfect, Mo thought. *Now's my chance. I have to take it.*

Mo scooted her chair up to April's desk and took a deep breath. "Hey, wanna be partners?" she asked.

Mo watched as April slowly took in her outfit and then finally settled on her face with a slight smile. "Sure, sounds good," she responded.

Relieved, Mo pulled her chair closer.

"So who are you friends with?" April asked directly, still scanning Mo's outfit. "I mean, I haven't really seen you hanging out with anyone."

Mo shifted uncomfortably in her chair. "Um, I'm not sure. . . . I guess I've been . . . kind of doing my own thing, you know?" She didn't think "well, I have no friends and making new friends hasn't really worked out" would be the kind of response April would want to hear.

"Who do you eat lunch with?" April asked abruptly.

Mo could feel her face heating up. "Um, I've been

kind of eating with different people . . . keeping my options open."

"Uh-huh," April said absentmindedly as she scribbled vocabulary words in her notebook.

Mo began to feel a little uncomfortable. There was something about April that she couldn't quite figure out. Not to mention that her outfit looked really expensive. Mo had seen shoes like April's at the mall and she couldn't believe how much they cost. She couldn't imagine spending that much money on a silly pair of shoes.

"Well, you should eat with me and my friends today. They're super cool, you'll like them," April said quickly and then went back to her notebook.

"OK!" Mo responded instantly. Maybe April was all right after all. *Maybe she's just nervous like me,* Mo thought. "Yeah, I didn't really have other plans yet, so that sounds good," Mo responded again, trying to play it cool. But April barely acknowledged her.

The rest of the morning seemed to pick up a little. Since Mo had lunch plans to look forward to, she didn't have to figure out where to hide so the Mean Ghouls wouldn't find her and broadcast her exile to the entire school. She skipped into the cafeteria right after history class and scanned the crowd for April's reddish-blond, long wavy hair. She found her in the corner of the room at a table already packed with other seventh and maybe even eighth graders, Mo wasn't sure. She approached the table a little slowly and waited for April to acknowledge her. *That's weird,* Mo thought to herself, *I thought this was Jenna and Stacia's table.* Mo looked around for the Mean Ghouls, but they were nowhere to be found.

"Oh, hey, Mo." April smiled, setting down her fork.

Mo shrugged off her uneasiness and set her backpack on the floor.

"Mo, this is Celeste, Samara, Todd, Carina, and Matthew." She pointed to each of the preppy faces at the table. Mo felt a couple of cold stares and lingering glances on her bob while the group took in her appearance. She stood awkwardly waiting for someone to make space for her to sit down.

"Is that an orange stain on your shirt?" Samara asked the minute Mo finally got settled. Mo could pretty much guess that there was indeed an orange stain on her shirt without even looking down. She had, after all, eaten an orange that very morning, and chances were that some of it had ended up on her clothes. That's just how things happened for Mo. She could hear her mother's voice in her head: "It's just an awkward phase, honey."

"Right," Mo said out loud.

"Huh?" Samara asked, crinkling her brow at Mo.

"So, what did you guys do over the summer?" Mo asked the group, trying to deflect attention from her orange stain and the fact that she had just been talking to herself.

Mo's question was met with deafening silence until April finally filled the space by telling Mo about her parents' beach house. As April talked, Mo glanced around the table and realized that no one else was even listening to the conversation anymore. They were all having conversations of their own, and ones that Mo wasn't so sure she wanted to be a part of.

"Did you see whatshername's outfit this morning?" Carina was saying. "I mean, hello, that look was *so* last year."

"And what about Annette Simon?" Todd added. "Those glasses are, like, from *The Jetsons* or something."

Mo felt that hollow feeling building up in the pit of her stomach again — the one she always felt when the Mean Ghouls were around.

"And what did you do this summer, Mo?" April asked, a sly smile spreading across her face. "Didn't you, like, shovel cow manure or something?"

The table erupted with laughter. Now everyone was definitely paying attention to Mo.

"What?" Mo stared at April. How did she . . . ?

"Hey, guys, sorry we're late!"

Mo turned in slow motion like she was in a horror movie about to come face-to-face with her zombie killer. And it was just as bad as that: Jenna, Stacia, and Gabby stood directly behind her chair.

"Oh, well, look who it is," Jenna blurted out. "How cute that you decided to take in the little hillbilly."

"I thought we might be able to help her learn to eat lunch like a normal person," April said in a condescending voice.

"That's so nice of you," Stacia giggled in her usual way.

"Except that now our table is going to smell like a farm," Gabby added.

"True," Jenna responded as everyone at the table exploded into laughter once again. Mo swept the contents of her lunch back inside the bag and stood up, letting the metal legs of her chair scrape loudly against the linoleum.

"You guys are just too mature for me," she said through the laughter. "Guess I'll be going."

Mo didn't even feel like crying this time. Mostly, she just felt defeated. *If girls like Jenna, Stacia, and Gabby can find that many new friends that quickly, how do I stand a chance?* she thought as she trudged down the hall toward her locker. *Guess their friend-worthy list was a success after all.* Suddenly, her pink (and orange-stained) polo shirt began to feel really itchy against her skin.

She searched the bottom of her locker and found the black T-shirt she had used for gym class the day before. It didn't smell too bad since all she had done was stand in the outfield and bat once. She grabbed the shirt and her backpack and headed for the bathroom to change.

On her way back down the hall, as she was trying to calculate whether or not she could actually fit herself inside her locker, Mo noticed a poster advertising a student-run clothing drive to raise money for charity. *That sounds kind of interesting,* she thought as she moved closer to investigate. Just then she heard a door squeak at the end of the hall and spotted a group of kids all dressed in black heading out the side door by the soccer field. At the other end of the hall, Mo saw the lunch monitor rounding the corner. Knowing that she needed to get out of the hall and avoid the monitor, Mo shrugged, glanced down at her black T-shirt, and decided to follow the group outside.

They were just getting settled in a patch of grass at the far edge of the soccer field as Mo approached. Several of them were listening to music on their headphones and most, if not all, of them were drawing or writing in journals. *This could be cool,* Mo thought to herself as she sat down on the grass and pulled on her skirt to cover more of her legs. She recognized Matt Bern from her science class, but no one else.

"What are you listening to?" she asked Matt, who looked startled to see her sitting ncxt to him.

He stared sideways at her through a thick slab of black hair. "Uh, probably nothing you've heard of," he replied before returning to his notebook.

The other students in the circle now realized Mo was there, but no one said a word to her, or to each other.

"Hi, I'm Mo," she said to the boy sitting next to Matt.

"Gabe," the boy answered without looking up from his sketch pad. He had almost finished a drawing of a giant winged dragon with a small boy clutched in its huge, jagged claws. Again several faces stared at Mo for a brief second before returning to their own books or papers.

"OK," Mo said aloud to herself. It was pretty clear

that no one was remotely interested in her and that maybe they were even a little annoyed that she had infiltrated their circle. Mo stood to leave and came face-to-face with the lunch monitor. She stood uncomfortably and tried to reach down for her backpack.

"Name, please," the lunch monitor said through gritted teeth. She held a pencil with its point pressed hard against an office pink slip.

"What? I was just going back inside," Mo protested weakly. "I didn't do anything."

"You most certainly did, young lady," the monitor responded, narrowing her brightly blue-shadowed eyes. "You are no longer on school grounds. You left school property without permission."

"But — but this is the soccer field. It belongs to the school!" Mo argued.

The monitor sighed loudly. "Do you see this fence line?"

Mo stared blankly in the direction she was pointing. "DO YOU?"

"Yeah, I guess."

"Well, you're outside of the line. Now, I don't have time to argue with you. The bell is about to ring and I need to write pink slips for every one of you. NAME, PLEASE."

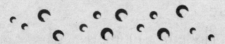

Mo slumped down in the chair outside the principal's office, clutching her pink slip to her stomach. Matt was next to her, doodling on the back of his.

"Sorry you got in trouble," he said, still doodling.

Mo was surprised to hear him speak. "It's not your fault. I'm the one who came out there."

"I know. But we're always getting in trouble from the lunch monster and you just didn't know."

"Lunch monster, that's a good one." Mo smiled.

"Thanks, that one's mine." Matt smiled back.

"Miss Solas, please come in." The principal had opened her door to let Gabe out.

"See ya," Matt said.

"Bye."

"So, Morgan." Mrs. Abbott sat down behind her desk and pointed to a chair for Mo. "I haven't seen you in my office since your first day of classes last year. I'm surprised to see you here today."

"Yeah." Mo couldn't think of any way to explain why she was there.

"Care to elaborate a bit more?" Mrs. Abbott smiled.

Mo knew right then she was going to cry and she really didn't want to. She had never been a "crier" in Maplewood. Sure, she would get upset — sometimes she and Libby would have a fight, or something would go wrong at school, but she felt like she had cried so much in Kirkland — she didn't even feel like herself anymore.

"It's just . . . I'm just . . . having a hard time this year, I guess," Mo mumbled as a big tear splashed onto her T-shirt.

Mrs. Abbott slid a box of tissues closer to Mo's side of the desk. "I'm really sorry to hear that, Morgan. You know that you can always come and talk to me."

"Thanks," Mo managed, grabbing a tissue to catch

the next tear. She found herself telling Mrs. Abbott all about trying to fit in with new groups and all the things that had happened that week. Mrs. Abbott laughed extra hard when Mo told her about *Drums for Dummies* and her almost–drum solo.

"I really admire you for making an effort to make new friends, Morgan. That's not an easy thing to do."

"Yeah, I've kind of started to realize that." Mo let out a small laugh.

"Well, I have all the faith in the world that you will find your place. You just have to be patient. And in the meantime, you're welcome to come to my office anytime you need to." Mrs. Abbott stood up.

"What about the pink slip?" Mo asked. "I really didn't know I was off school grounds."

"Don't worry about that. I think it was an honest mistake." Mrs. Abbott winked at Mo. "Now, take some time if you need to freshen up in the girls' bathroom and then have Mrs. Velasquez write you a pass to class, all right?"

CHAPTER 7
Pep Talks

MO FELT A MIXTURE of relief and misery as she waited
for the bus on Friday morning. Her talk with Mrs.
Abbott had made her feel a little better about things,
but the idea of facing another morning of the Mean
Ghouls and their nasty routine was almost too much.
Then again, Mo was relieved that it was the end of the
week and she had a weekend away from school, but
the fact that she didn't have a single plan to look
forward to for the weekend was miserable.

When the bus door slid open and Mo climbed inside,
she almost shouted for joy when neither Jenna's nor
Stacia's witchy expression glared back at her from the

girls' usual lair. *They must have convinced Jenna's mom to drive them,* Mo thought as she bounced toward an empty seat. Joey wasn't on the bus either, so that was further proof they'd gotten a ride. Mo settled in and enjoyed her first relaxing bus ride of the school year.

The rest of her day went just as smoothly. Mo brought her bag lunch to the library and settled into a corner with her worn copy of *A Wrinkle in Time.* She didn't have gym this Friday because of some locker room maintenance, so there was no chance of getting stuck on a team with Stacia and Gabby or being yelled at by the competitive AAs. She didn't see Joey all day, but she didn't see the Mean Ghouls either. As her bus pulled away from the school that afternoon, she spotted Stan and Christine across the parking lot. *I should have asked for their numbers to get a slice of pizza this weekend,* Mo thought to herself, realizing that she had practically forgotten about the good time they had had after her embarrassing marching band fiasco.

At home Mo remembered Alexa's plea earlier that

week to stay the night at Jenny's house. She was glad to have the house to herself, but annoyed again that Alexa had plans and she didn't. Mo quickly ate a snack of crackers and cheese in the kitchen and went up to her room to call Libby.

"Oh, good, I'm glad you caught me before I left," Libby said when she answered the phone.

"Where are you going?"

"Michilene is having a girl-boy party for her birthday tonight, so I'm going over early to help with the decorations and stuff."

"Oh." Mo crumpled onto her bed. She had hoped that Libby didn't have plans either so they could just hang out and chat for hours since she didn't have to worry about Alexa and the phone.

"What are you doing tonight?" Libby asked to fill the silence.

"Nothing."

"How was the rest of your week?" Libby probed again, hopefully. "Did you try talking to that preppy girl?"

"Yeah. Turns out she's friends with the Mean Ghouls, so that didn't go so well."

"You're kidding!"

"Nope."

"Mo, I'm sorry."

"It's all right. I'm kind of getting used to hanging out by myself."

"No, don't say that!" Libby pleaded. "I know you're going to find the right group — you just have to give it more time. It's only been a week."

"Yeah, easy for you to say," Mo argued.

"I know, I know. I just don't want you to give up, because you're the most amazing friend I have and I know there are plenty of people at your school who will think that, too, when they get to know you," Libby responded.

"Thanks. I keep trying to tell myself that, but it's hard. I never expected it to be like this." Mo fought back tears for the millionth time that week.

"It will get better, you'll see." Libby tried to sound as

upbeat as possible. "And let's start planning which weekend I should come for a visit! I'm dying to see your room all done up and stuff. You were barely unpacked last time I was there."

"Yeah, let's definitely start planning," Mo responded, brightening a little at the thought of seeing Libby. "You're going to love my room! I found this chair —"

"Shoot, Michilene's mom is here to pick me up. I'm sorry I can't talk longer. And I wish you could come tonight! Mark Aronson is totally going to be there!"

"I really wish I could, too." Mo sighed. "Well, call me tomorrow and tell me everything."

"For sure! Bye!"

"Bye."

On Saturday, Mo spent the day reading, doing homework, and helping her mom organize her office. That night, Alexa was home, surprisingly with no plans, so the two girls watched movies with their parents.

After the second movie ended and Mo's parents said good night, Mo was set to grab the popcorn bowl to take it to the kitchen and then head up to her room.

"So how's Emerson this year and stuff?" Alexa asked before Mo could get up from the couch.

Mo set the bowl back on the coffee table and fidgeted with the hem of her pajama pants. "Um, it's all right."

"Did you try out for marching band or something?" Alexa asked with a confused look on her face.

"I, well, almost, but not really. It's a long story," Mo stumbled. She couldn't believe that even Alexa had somehow heard about that. "So how's fourth grade?" She was ready to change the subject.

"It's good. I like it so far. I miss Maplewood, though."

"Really?" Mo was surprised. "You never talk about Maplewood. I thought you didn't miss it at all."

"I do miss it," Alexa argued. "I miss my old school and I miss the orchard."

"I guess I didn't realize," Mo responded. "You seem so happy here and you have so many friends. . . ."

"I do like it here. And I have made more friends here than I thought I'd ever have, but that doesn't mean I don't miss stuff about Maplewood, too," Alexa said, looking tentatively at Mo. "Is everything OK with you? You seem weird lately."

Mo sighed. "I'm not having the greatest year so far."

Alexa stared at her expectantly. Mo was hoping to leave it at that, but Alexa clearly wasn't going anywhere.

"I'm not friends with Jenna and Stacia anymore. We had a huge fight," Mo said finally. She watched Alexa's eyes grow wider. "I finally realized they weren't the kind of friends I wanted to have, I guess."

"Geez," Alexa replied. "I had no idea."

"And it's been a lot harder than I thought it would be to find other friends, you know?" Mo looked at Alexa. "Well, I guess you don't know."

"What's that supposed to mean?"

"You obviously haven't had any problem finding friends here, Alexa." Mo could feel herself getting kind of annoyed. She hated even having this conversation with her *little* sister.

"Maybe not, but I never had friends in Maplewood like you did," Alexa said, seeming a little annoyed herself. "You and Libby have been friends for, like, ever and I was always jealous of that. I wanted a best friend like that, too, and I never found one until we moved here."

Mo stared back at Alexa. She had no idea Alexa had been jealous of her friendship with Libby. She thought nothing bothered her. "I didn't realize . . ." was all Mo could think to say.

"I'm sorry about Jenna and Stacia," Alexa responded. "But I'm kinda glad you aren't friends with them anymore. They always treated me like a baby."

Mo thought for a minute. "Yeah, I don't know why it took me so long to realize what jerks they are."

"One time when they were staying over last year, Jenna tried to lock me in the hall closet," Alexa added.

Mo stared back at her. "Are you serious?"

"Yep."

Both girls looked at each other for a minute and then burst into laughter. Mo fell sideways on the couch and clutched her stomach. She could barely catch her breath, she was laughing so hard. Alexa slipped onto the floor, her shoulders shaking against the back of the recliner.

Once they were finally able to stop laughing, Alexa looked up at Mo. "I know you'll find the friends you want here. The whole seventh-grade class would have to be crazy not to want to be friends with you, Mo."

Mo smiled back at Alexa. That was the nicest thing she had ever said. "Thanks. And sorry I've been a little snippy lately."

"That's OK, I'm getting used to it," Alexa replied with a grin.

On Sunday, Mo tried to have a better attitude and think of something fun to do. She was about to ask Alexa if she wanted to go to a movie or play a game, but Alexa already had plans to go to the mall with her BFF Jenny. As soon as Alexa skipped out the door to meet her friend, Mo slumped into a bad mood again. She moped around the house all morning until her mom came up to her room, holding her purse and car keys.

"Come on," she said, gesturing toward the door with her head.

"Where?" Mo was sprawled out on her bed staring at the ceiling.

"We're going to visit Grandma."

"Mom," Mo whined. "I really don't feel like it right now."

Now that her grandma needed care at a home, Mo felt uncomfortable every time she saw her. Mo had always gotten along great with her grandma and usually loved seeing her, but ever since they moved to Kirkland last year and her grandmother had moved into Shady Pines, Mo had a hard time visiting her. Mo didn't like to think about her grandma being older or getting sick.

"Well, too bad. Grandma wants to see you and you need to get out of this house and stop moping around." Mrs. Solas put her hand on her hip. Clearly, she meant business.

"Fine." Mo peeled herself off her bed and put on her shoes.

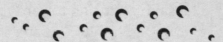

As soon as Mo and Mrs. Solas pulled up at Shady Pines, Mo began to feel nervous.

Inside, Mo's mom motioned her toward her grandmother's room and said, "You go on in. I need to talk to the administrator for a minute."

Mo gave her mom a look but knew she couldn't argue. She started walking as slowly as possible toward her grandmother's room. She knocked lightly on the door, hoping maybe her grandma was sleeping or having her hair done or something.

"Come in."

Mo turned the doorknob and peeked cautiously inside, as if she were unsure what she might find on the other side of the door.

"MoMo!" Mo's grandmother cried. She set aside her crochet project and stood up, ready to give Mo a hug.

"Hi, Grandma," Mo said shakily.

"Well, get over here and give me a hug!"

Mo moved unsteadily toward her grandmother and stood in front of her. Her grandma grabbed her waist and drew her in for a giant hug. Mo couldn't believe how strong she seemed.

"Come sit over by the window with me, Mo. I just came in from a walk and the air is so wonderful today."

Mo started to relax a little and joined her grandma by the open window, which looked out onto a huge manicured lawn.

Mo's grandma took Mo's hands and placed them on her lap. "So I want to hear all about your first week of seventh grade. How are your friends? Are there any cute boys?" she said with a wink.

Mo laughed and relaxed even more. This was the grandma she was used to. She didn't know why she had been so worried.

"It wasn't such a good week, Gram," Mo said, looking into her grandmother's concerned eyes. "I'm not really friends with Jenna and Stacia anymore and I'm kind of having a hard time making new friends."

"I find that so hard to believe, honey," Mo's grandma replied. "You always had a million friends in Maplewood. There were always kids running around the orchard ready to play."

"Yeah, I guess it's just different here. I don't know."

Mo sat back in her chair and told her grandma all about her week. Mo's grandma took up her crocheting again and listened quietly, nodding or shaking her head where appropriate. Mo didn't leave out a single detail. She told her grandma about the bus rides, the lunch tables, marching band, gym class, the principal's office, and even about Joey.

When Mo was finally done, she let out a huge breath. It felt so good to be here and to talk to her grandma.

"Well, honey." Mo's grandma set down her crocheting again and looked at Mo seriously. "It does sound like you've had a hard week, but it also sounds like you've made plenty of friends!"

"What?" Mo was totally confused, and then worried.

Maybe her grandma wasn't doing as well as she thought. Had she heard *anything* Mo just said?

"You've got Stan and Christine to get pizza with after school or go to the football games with. You've got Jordan to come over and play basketball in the driveway. You've got Annette to help you with your math homework, or for you to go with to the salon. And this girl Nicole and this boy Joey both sound like very nice kids. I bet either one of them would be thrilled to spend a Saturday with you."

Mo let her grandmother's words sink in a little bit before she spoke again.

"You're totally right, Gram," Mo said, smiling. "I didn't even see it, but you're right." Then Mo launched herself toward her grandmother and gave her a huge hug.

Her grandmother laughed. "See, I'm not so old that I can't still teach you a thing or two!"

"Thanks, Gram," Mo said with an answering laugh.

"I don't like seeing you so down like that, Morgan," her grandmother responded seriously. "You need to always remember what a wonderful young lady you are. Don't let a couple of bad apples make you think you're not."

"I know," Mo said quietly.

"You can come see me whenever you want, you know. Even if your mom is busy, the bus stops right at the corner."

"I'm sorry I haven't visited more, Gram. I totally will!" Mo answered eagerly. She knew it had been silly to be nervous about coming to Shady Pines.

Mo's mom knocked quickly on the door and let herself in. "What did I miss?"

Her grandma and Mo both laughed and said, "Oh, nothing."

Mo and her mom spent the rest of the afternoon hanging out with Mo's grandma. She started to teach Mo to crochet and then Mo's mom went over a few bills and prescriptions with her before they said good-bye. As they walked back down the hall toward the entrance, Mo saw a familiar face. Standing near the front reception desk was Nicole and another girl who looked their age.

"Mom, I'll catch up to you at the car — there's a girl from school I want to say hi to."

Mo's mom smiled and squeezed Mo's shoulder. "Sounds good."

"Hey, Mo! What are you doing here?" Nicole smiled.

"My grandma lives here. I was just visiting her with my mom. What are you doing here?"

"Mela and I volunteer here," Nicole replied, gesturing toward her friend. "This is Mela. She goes to Emerson, too. Mela, this is Mo."

"Nice to meet you!" Mela responded with an equally friendly smile.

"Nice to meet you, too." Mo smiled back. "That's so great you guys are volunteers."

"Yeah, we come one Sunday a month to hang out with the residents and do projects and stuff — it's really fun!" said Mela.

"Wow, that does sound like fun! Well, my grandma

is in room 122, so be sure to be extra nice to her!" Mo added.

Nicole and Mela responded with a laugh. "We will for sure."

Mo gave a quick wave and another smile. "See you at school tomorrow!"

Mo climbed into the car and buckled her seat belt. "Thanks, Mom. I'm really glad we came."

"Good." Mrs. Solas smiled. "So, who were those girls?"

"They're in my class at Emerson. They volunteer here," Mo responded.

"That's nice. You should ask if you can join them. Grandma would be so excited to see you there more often."

"Good idea. I don't know why I didn't think of that!" Mo slapped her hand to her forehead.

"Well, you'll just have to talk to them about it at school." Mo's mom smiled again.

"Yeah, I guess so."

CHAPTER 8
Clueless

MO HAD FELT GREAT when she went to bed Sunday night. She had a whole new outlook on things, thanks to her grandma. Monday morning, however, was a different story. Her alarm didn't go off. When she got blasted with cold water in the shower, she slipped and banged her knee against the side of the tub. As she sprinted her way down the stairs to try to catch the bus, she missed a step and crashed onto the same knee — this time tearing a hole in her favorite jeans. By the time Mo got back downstairs after finding a Band-Aid for her knee and a clean pair of pants, she had missed the bus. So much for her sunny outlook from the day before!

Luckily, she was able to catch her dad on his way out the door and get a ride to school. Mo couldn't stand the classical music her father always listened to in the car, but at least she didn't have to face the Mean Ghouls on the bus.

Mo ran from the parking lot to her locker, thinking she still had a chance to beat the final bell. When she opened her locker (on the third try this time — at least she was improving), a massive pile of hay fell out on top of her.

Before Mo even knew what it was that had fallen on her, a large crowd began to form around her locker. People were laughing and pointing and gawking. Then, as if by magic, the crowd parted and the Mean Ghouls emerged to make barnyard jokes and hillbilly jabs. Mo just stood there, frozen. *How did they even get my locker open?* she wondered. *They must have sweet-talked the janitor or something,* she thought as she tried to remove her backpack from the pile of hay around her feet.

When the final bell rang, the crowd disappeared as

quickly as it had formed and left Mo standing alone, picking pieces of hay from her hair and clothes. Just then Mrs. Abbott and Mrs. Velasquez appeared from around the corner.

"Oh, Morgan," Mrs. Abbott gasped. "Mrs. Velasquez, will you please call Mr. Peterson and ask him to bring a broom and some cleaning supplies?"

"Yes, right away," Mrs. Velasquez replied, trying to stifle a laugh.

"Morgan." Mrs. Abbott turned toward Mo and tried to help brush some of the hay from her back. "Who did this?"

"It's fine, Mrs. Abbott" was all Mo could say. She didn't think getting Jenna and Stacia into trouble was really going to help her at this point.

"Well, go clean up and then go directly to your first class. I'll let your homeroom teacher know you are here. And if you determine who is behind this, you come and see me," she replied with a knowing look.

All Mo wanted was to get through the day without another person pointing and whispering about the hay incident. Luckily, her English class had independent reading time to prepare for their research reports, so no group interaction there. The last thing Mo wanted was for April to be able to continue the joke during class. In history, however, Mr. Hayes separated the class into groups for a biography project. Mo was paired with two girls, Sophie and Hannah. The girls seemed nice enough at first and didn't seem to recognize Mo as the "hillbilly from the hall." Unfortunately, they were also a little clueless about other things. While Mo began to do Internet research on their biography subject, the two girls debated rather seriously about which nail polish was the best color for celebrities to wear on the red carpet. Whenever Mo tried to get them to focus on the project or asked them a question to get them involved, they just complimented Mo on the great job she was doing and returned to their discussion.

By the end of class, Mo had practically completed the project on her own.

"Uh, guys, I'm almost done with this. Are you sure you have nothing to add?" Mo sighed with frustration.

"Wow, Mo, nice work!" was Sophie's reply.

"Yeah, great job!" Hannah added.

As annoyed as Mo was, and as much as she didn't think "clueless" was one of the groups she had planned to include in her friendship experiment, when the two girls asked Mo to join them for lunch, she agreed. At least having someone to eat lunch with would keep her mind off of the Mean Ghouls and hopefully create a buffer against their teasing.

In the cafeteria, Mo sat with Hannah and Sophie at a table in the front of the room, near the hot-lunch line. The two girls now argued about which contestant on last night's reality show was cuter: the mean athlete guy or the nice dog trainer guy. Mo tried to interject what few comments she could, but it was a little tough to follow their conversation, which veered off onto topics such as whether Hannah could wear the color lavender with her skin tone and if Sophie had been born in the 1800s, would her name still be Sophie.

Toward the end of the lunch period, as Mo was contemplating trying to get in trouble with Matt Bern's group again just so she'd have something to do, Mo realized that Mela and Nicole were eating lunch three tables away. She hadn't seen them at lunch at all the week before. *That's weird,* Mo thought, *maybe they switched lunch periods.* She was just about to make an excuse to Hannah and Sophie so she could go say hi to them when Hannah grabbed her arm.

"Come on, Mo, lunch is about to end and I could really use your help with my math homework — it's due sixth period."

"Yeah, me, too!" Sophie responded. "I just don't get it."

Mo glanced toward Nicole and Mela's table. "Uh . . . actually," she started to say, but Hannah jerked harder on her arm and Sophie pushed her toward the door.

Somehow either Sophie or Hannah or both girls managed to find Mo between every class that afternoon to ask her for help. Sophie even asked Mo if she would spend her study hall finishing Sophie's Spanish homework. When Mo explained that she didn't even take Spanish, Sophie's reply was, "That's OK, it's not like I know any of the words either."

By the end of the day, Mo was exhausted. As she headed to her bus, Hannah and Sophie found her one last time.

"Mo!" Hannah called, jogging toward her. "Do you want to come over to my house?"

Mo thought for a brief moment about whether or not she could handle being friends with such clueless girls when Hannah added: "Sophie and I have these English reports due next week and we could really use your help!"

By that point, Mo had had it. She realized that Sophie and Hannah didn't care about being friends with her. They just wanted someone to do all their schoolwork for them.

"Yeah, sounds tempting," Mo managed, trying not to get angry. "But I have my own homework to do. I gotta go."

Mo dashed onto the bus, took the first seat behind the driver, sank down, and put on her headphones. All she wanted was to be invisible.

That night while Mo did her homework, she and Libby instant-messaged each other online. Libby gave Mo details from Michilene's party on Friday night. Then she described her sleepover with a whole different group of girls on Saturday night. Mo tried not to be too down in her responses. She was glad Libby was having such a good time, but she worried that Libby might start to forget her with all these other friends in her life.

After Libby finished describing her weekend, she wanted an update on Mo's weekend and her Monday, too. Mo quickly told Libby about the hay incident and about her afternoon tutoring Hannah and Sophie. She didn't feel like dwelling on it too much. She was starting to get angry just thinking about it again. Then she told Libby about spending time with her grandmother and about seeing Nicole and Mela at Shady Pines. Libby suggested that Mo ask the girls if she could volunteer at Shady Pines. Mo laughed out loud and explained to Libby that her mother had suggested the same thing.

I guess I'm a little slow 2 the party, Mo typed.

U just have 2 ask them tmrw, Libby responded.

Mo knew she was right.

Then Alexa burst into Mo's room and pleaded with her for the laptop.

"I *haaave* to use it!" she cried. "Jenny and I are working on a project and Alli and Emily are in a fight again and I'm supposed to IM with all of them in, like, two minutes!"

Mo sighed. "Fine, just let me say good-bye to Libby."

Libby and Mo chatted for a few more minutes, just to annoy Alexa, and then Mo logged off and handed over the laptop. Alexa dashed out of the room as if her life depended on it. Mo was kind of relieved that her interactions with Alexa were back to normal. It would be too weird if they started being really friendly toward each other.

Mo flopped down on her bed and stared up at the ceiling. She thought about the day she wasted spending time with Hannah and Sophie. Clearly, her friendship experiment had not gone the way she wanted it to. Then she replayed the hay incident in her mind. All the teasing and taunting from Jenna and Stacia had not gone away either. Mo decided that the next day she would try a different approach with the Mean Ghouls. Instead of trying to ignore them, it was time to stand up to them and let them know just how tired of them she was. She also decided maybe it was time to abandon her experiment and just try to work with the new friends she had already made. She would invite Christine and Stan out for pizza. She would ask Annette if she wanted to go to the mall and get her hair cut. And she would ask Mela and Nicole about volunteering at Shady Pines. It was time to take action!

CHAPTER 9
A New Project

THE NEXT MORNING, Mo was totally prepared to confront Jenna and Stacia on the bus, so of course they weren't on it. When Mo got to her locker, she steadied herself and even jumped back a little when she opened the door, on the second try this time, but nothing was there. In homeroom, Mo arrived a little early so she'd have a chance to talk to Annette.

"Hey, Annette," she said as she slid into her desk.

"Hi!" Annette peered back from behind her black glasses with rhinestones on the frames.

"I like your glasses."

"Thanks! I just got them last night." Annette smiled.

"So I was thinking, if you still wanted to get your hair cut, we could go to the mall this weekend," Mo offered.

"Oh, yeah, I forgot about that. Actually, with my new glasses I think I want to keep my hair long," Annette replied, smoothing her hand down her hair. "Thanks, though!"

"Oh. OK, sure." Annette's response caught Mo by surprise. She had thought for sure she'd finally have a plan for the weekend.

Just then Mrs. Lawrence asked the class to quiet down and began the morning announcements. Mo glanced toward the back of the room and met Nicole's eye. Nicole gave a little wave. *I should ask her about volunteering at Shady Pines,* Mo thought, remembering both her mom's and Libby's suggestions. *But why hasn't Nicole tried to talk to me?* she wondered. *They probably don't need any more volunteers,* she decided, *or they would have asked me right away. She probably already has her set group of friends, too.* Mo felt even more unsure of herself now.

On her way to her locker after English class, Mo stopped to get a drink at the water fountain and was cornered by the Mean Ghouls.

"Look who it is, girls." Jenna glowered. "It's the hillbilly in the hall."

"I thought I smelled cow manure," Stacia sneered.

"Yeah —" Gabby started, but Mo interrupted.

"You know what," she said in the voice that seemed to startle all three girls. "I know you guys think you're being really funny and that you're totally getting to me and making my life miserable, but the truth is I really don't care."

Jenna's eyes widened and she started to say something in retaliation.

"You can save it, Jenna." Mo held up her hand. "Really, I don't care what you have to say. I just want you to know that you can continue to bully me and be as mean as you have been, but it's not going to affect me. All I know is that I'm just glad I'm not wasting any more of my time being friends with mean girls like you."

And with that, Mo continued toward her locker. She sneaked a quick peek backward and saw that all three girls were still standing by the water fountain. Jenna seemed to be ranting about something, but Stacia looked a little shaken up, and Gabby definitely seemed upset. *Maybe Gabby's feeling a little unsure about her friendship choice now,* Mo thought.

As lunchtime approached, Mo didn't know what to do. Should she eat alone in the library or go to the computer lab? Should she try to approach Nicole and Mela's table? But what if they weren't there? She had only seen them in the cafeteria one time. Mo decided to brave the cafeteria and just keep her fingers crossed that Nicole and Mela were there. She had to at least ask them about Shady Pines, otherwise she wasn't being true to her experiment. She entered the doorway to the lunchroom and frantically scanned the tables, looking for their friendly faces. She saw Annette and her friends having a heated debate about something.

She saw Hannah and Sophie poring over a fashion magazine. She saw Jordan and the AAs demonstrating some sort of basketball technique. And she saw the Mean Ghouls and their entourage huddled in the corner, whispering and glaring at the room. But she didn't see Nicole and Mela. Mo was about to dart back into the hall and retreat to the library when she decided it was time to live up to what she had just told Jenna, Stacia, and Gabby. They were not going to affect her anymore. If she had to eat lunch by herself and risk being humiliated in front of the entire lunchroom, so be it.

Mo took a seat at an empty table near the door and opened her lunch bag. She took a notebook and a pen from her bag and decided to busy herself by writing a letter to Libby. She and Libby tried hard to send packages and letters to each other in addition to all their e-mails and phone calls because it was so much fun to get something in the mail when you least expected it. Mo thought she noticed Jenna pointing in her direction at one point, but the rest of her table seemed to be focused on something else. Mo smiled in spite of herself. Maybe her new plan was working after all.

Just before science lab, Mo decided to check the band room, hoping to find Christine and Stan. Even though it hadn't worked out to make plans with Annette, she felt sure Christine and Stan would be up for hanging out. Just as she predicted, they were practicing their instruments.

"Hey, guys," Mo said cheerfully.

"Hi, Mo," Christine replied. "We haven't seen you around much."

"Yeah," Stan added, "we thought maybe you switched schools or something after that hay incident."

Christine punched Stanley in the arm and gave him a look.

Mo laughed. "No, I've just been busy, I guess. Hey, I was going to see if you guys wanted to get pizza after school one day this week."

"I wish we could," said Christine.

"Yeah, we really can't," Stan chimed in. "We have band practice every day after school now."

"Oh." Mo deflated a little bit. "Well, just thought I'd ask."

"Thanks, though!" Christine replied. "If we ever get a break from practice, we'll definitely let you know."

"Yeah, like that's ever gonna happen." Stanley laughed, and Christine shot him another look.

"Well, maybe on the weekend, then, or something," Mo suggested.

"Ugh, weekends are even worse!" Stan replied.

Christine glared at Stan even harder. "We have two big games to get ready for this weekend and next, but after that, we should definitely do something."

"OK, yeah," Mo said quietly as she turned toward the door. "See you guys later."

In study hall, Mo asked for a pass to the computer lab. She was supposed to be working on her English report, but she spent the entire period researching other middle schools in the Kirkland area. She figured if she could convince her parents to move just ten blocks east, she could transfer to T. R. Bailey Middle School. Maybe if she just started over completely, she'd have better luck finding friends.

By the end of the day, the confidence Mo had felt from standing up to the Mean Ghouls and proving she could eat lunch alone in the cafeteria had disappeared completely. She started to feel like her situation was totally hopeless. She had tried to work with the friends she'd already made, but it seemed as if everyone was too busy doing their own thing to make time for her. It was too late. Everyone already *had* all the friends they wanted. Mo wandered down the hall toward the parking lot in a complete daze. She started drafting the argument she planned to make to her parents about transferring to Bailey. She even stopped to dig a piece of paper out of her bag so she could write down some notes.

"*Psssst.*"

Mo looked in front of her and the hall was empty. She glanced behind her and there were just two girls walking in the opposite direction.

"Psssst, Mo."

She even looked above her, worried for a second that the Mean Ghouls had managed to rig some sort of prank in the ceiling, in that exact spot.

"Mo! In here!" Mo looked to her left and realized she was standing outside an open classroom and there was a group of students inside. She approached the door cautiously and peered in. Joey, Nicole, Mela, and several other students Mo didn't know were sitting there. Most of them had notebooks open on their desks and Nicole had a laptop in front of her.

"Hi," Mo said in a small voice.

"Come in." Joey smiled and motioned Mo toward the desk next to his.

"What are you guys doing in here?" Mo asked.

"This is our volunteer group," Nicole answered. "The one I was telling you about when I saw you at Shady Pines on Sunday."

"Oh . . ." Mo was still a little confused.

"Yeah, we organized the Emerson Student Volunteer Group last spring," Joey explained. "We've been meeting in Mr. Sand's room after school and also at lunch lately because we have so many events and stuff to plan for."

"We volunteer at the animal shelter and Shady Pines, but we also get hired by businesses to organize charity events and fund-raisers," Mela added.

"Wow." Mo was amazed. "That sounds really cool."

"Want to join us?" Nicole asked.

"Um, are you sure? I mean, yeah, if you guys have room for me. . . ." Mo stumbled over her words.

"Totally!" Joey said enthusiastically, blushing slightly.

"We always need more people," one girl chimed in. "We have so much to do!"

"Then, yes, I would love to!" Mo beamed from ear to ear.

Mo slid into the desk next to Joey.

"Like Joey said, we've had to meet at lunch a lot lately," Mela explained. "Does that work OK for you?"

"Definitely." Mo laughed. "I think I can squeeze it in."

"Great," Nicole responded. "We were just having a quick recap of our clothing drive from last week."

"I saw a poster for that in the hallway yesterday. It sounded cool," Mo said as she settled in.

"It went really well and we had tons of fun!" Nicole added.

The meeting got back under way and Mo listened quietly as each member of the group recapped their role in the clothing drive. It was clear that everyone had had a great time being involved in the drive and that it had been very successful. Everyone laughed and joked. It was easy to see that they were all friends.

CHAPTER 10
Mo's Idea

AS MO WAITED FOR THE BUS the next morning, she felt like a totally different person. Nicole, Mela, Joey, and the others in the Emerson Student Volunteer Group seemed genuinely excited to have her involved. She had given everyone her phone number and e-mail address so that she could be included in the group correspondence and start adding her ideas to the mix. She hadn't even glared at Jeremy that morning when he finished all the orange juice in one gulp. And it didn't seem to bother her quite so much when Alexa got three phone calls from her friends before eight A.M. When the bus pulled up and Joey wasn't on it but

Jenna and Stacia were, Mo didn't mind. She even smiled and shook her head a little when the only empty seat was directly in front of theirs. Mo sat down and took out her English report to check for mistakes one last time.

"Great," Mo heard Jenna say. "Now my new sweater is totally going to smell like a cow pasture by the time we get to school."

"Jenna, don't," Stacia replied. Mo lifted her head in surprise.

"Don't *what*?" Jenna asked dramatically.

"Just don't, OK?" Stacia sighed and turned toward the window.

Mo smiled and went back to her English paper. That was the first time she had ever heard Stacia stand up to Jenna. Mo enjoyed the silence all the way to Emerson.

"OK, guys, let's get down to business," Nicole said as she rapped her pencil against the side of her laptop screen. Everybody settled into their seats and got out their folders and notebooks.

"So, first we need to add Mo to our schedule for visiting Shady Pines," Nicole said, pulling up a spreadsheet of dates and times. "Also, since Mela is going to be taking over the animal shelter project, we will need a new volunteer leader for Shady Pines."

Mela turned toward Mo to explain. "Each volunteer project has a leader — someone who's in charge of communicating with the organization and handling schedule changes and stuff."

"That's great," Mo responded.

"So, would you want to be the new volunteer leader for Shady Pines?" Nicole asked.

"I would love to!" Mo smiled. "I mean, if that's OK with everyone else."

"I've already got the highway cleanup project, so go for it!" Mike replied.

"Totally," Shandra answered. "I've got the clothing drive."

"And I'm working on starting an after-school tutoring project at the elementary school," Joey explained.

"Great. Looks like Mo's our new Shady Pines leader." Nicole smiled as she updated the information on her laptop.

"My grandma's going to be very excited about this," said Mo. "And I'm sure she won't be shy about giving her suggestions either."

The group laughed.

"So the next item on our agenda is that we just got an e-mail on our Web site this morning from Abigail Cherington," Nicole continued. "She's the Kirkland representative of the biggest cancer fund-raising organization in the country and she wants us to help plan the Kirkland branch's annual charity event. She even wants us to propose some ideas for it!" Nicole finished excitedly.

"Wow. This could be big for us!" said Mela.

"What should we do? Does anybody have any ideas?" Joey asked.

The group sat quietly for a while. Slowly a few ideas started to bubble to the surface.

"What about a carnival?" Spencer asked.

"Too expensive," Mela responded. "We looked into that last spring for another event."

"How about a bake sale?" said Shandra.

"I thought about that," Nicole added, "but we've done that before. I think we need something more exciting for such a big event."

The group tossed around a few more ideas and Mo sat quietly, trying to think of something fun and original. Since this was her first official after-school meeting as part of the group, she really wanted to impress everyone. She couldn't believe how much her confidence had begun to come back. From the minute she had walked into Mr. Sand's room and found the friends she was looking for, everything had changed. She finally felt completely at ease. The group wasn't arguing about Latin or physics. They weren't talking in musical terms she didn't understand. They weren't making fun of anyone. And they weren't superathletes or tortured artists. Mo couldn't believe how well she fit in here and that the friends she'd been trying so hard to meet had been right under her nose the entire time.

Suddenly, she had it. "What about a barn dance!" she shouted out. "We can sell tickets to the dance and everyone can dress up in Western outfits and we can have square dancing and a country band."

"That's a great idea!" Joey replied excitedly.

Nicole typed furiously on her keyboard. "We could collect tickets and have a refreshment table and a coat check and everything. I love it!"

"It's perfect," Mela added. "We could sell lemonade and iced tea and make corn bread and chili and other fun snacks."

The other group members all nodded excitedly in agreement and added a few ideas of their own.

"Ms. Cherington wanted us to call her as soon as we came up with an idea, so let's call her and let her know our proposal!" Nicole jumped up and rushed over to Mr. Sand's desk. She dialed the number and looked nervous as she waited for Ms. Cherington to pick up. The rest of the group stared intently at Nicole as she spoke. Mo's heart was beating a million times a minute. She really wanted Ms. Cherington to like her idea. It would be so much fun to plan.

"Yes, that's a great idea," Nicole said into the phone, giving an excited thumbs-up to the rest of the group. "OK, that sounds great. OK, we'll give you a call at the end of the week, then." Nicole hung up the phone. "She loved it! She said she can't wait to start working out all of the details!"

Everyone was out of their chairs and jumping around excitedly.

"She even suggested that we talk to Mrs. Abbott about holding the event here at Emerson so students and their families would buy tickets and come, too!"

Mo couldn't believe how quickly her idea was turning into a huge event. Now everyone in the school would be talking about it.

"Great idea, Mo!" said Mela.

"Totally!" Spencer agreed as everyone patted Mo on the back.

Joey gave Mo a huge smile. "Yeah, nice work."

After the meeting, Mo and her new friends headed out to the school parking lot, where the last buses were loading up. Nicole, Mela, and Joey were all coming to Mo's house to continue planning the barn dance. Mo couldn't help but think about Jenna, Stacia, and Gabby. They were going to flip out when they heard about the dance and that it was Mo's idea. There was no way anyone would care about all their dumb small-town farm jokes after a really fun barn dance. A smile widened across Mo's face.

"We definitely need to get some hay bales to put in the gym," she suggested.

Joey, Mela, and Nicole all laughed.

"Yeah, maybe Jenna might know where we can get some," Joey said.

"She does seem to be an expert on the stuff," Nicole responded.

"We should offer to hire her to be our hay keeper for the dance," Mela added, their laughter growing louder.

"How are you related to her, Joey?" Nicole joked.

"Hey, don't blame me! I think she's an alien twin."

Mo hadn't felt this happy in a long time — in over a year, in fact. While her experiment hadn't exactly gone the way she'd imagined it would, she had ended up with the best friends she could possibly hope for (well, except for Libby, of course). And Libby! She couldn't wait to introduce her new friends to Libby. Mo knew they would all get along super well.

Mo noticed Nicole and Mela speeding up toward the open door of the late bus. She was about to quicken her pace when she felt Joey's hand touch her arm. He was hanging back slightly and Mo noticed his cheeks beginning to flush.

"So I was, um, wondering if maybe you'd want to see a movie on Saturday night . . . with me?" Joey said quietly, staring at the pavement.

Mo's heart raced. "Sure!" she blurted out excitedly. "I mean, yeah, that sounds cool," she added, trying to sound more casual.

Joey grinned, blushing even more. "OK, cool."

"Come on, slowpokes," Mela laughed from the door of the bus.

Just as Mo was about to step inside, Joey stopped her again. She turned toward him, a goofy grin still plastered on her face.

"And you better save me a square dance at the fund-raiser," Joey said quickly, trying to get it out before he lost his nerve.

Mo nodded and replied yes with a long, slow "*Mooooooooooo!*" before skipping up the bus steps to join her new friends.